EYES EVERYWHERE

SEARCHING FOR JEWISH CHILDREN

Also by Colleen Clancy Hansen:

Destination: Butte, Montana, a memoir

Ghost Children in Elkhorn, Montana, an eBook

Stella and the Bubble Man, a picture book

EYES EVERYWHERE

SEARCHING FOR
JEWISH CHILDREN

COLLEEN CLANCY HANSEN

MOUNTAIN PINE PRESS

ISBN: 979-8-9899009-5-4
ISBN (eBook): 979-8-9899009-6-1

Eyes Everywhere: Searching for Jewish Children

Cover by Mountain Pine Press. Image of Ha'penny Bridge by Colleen Clancy Hansen.

https://www.mountainpinepress.com
Helena, Montana

Published in the United States of America

DEDICATION

Eyes Everywhere: Searching for Jewish Children is written in remembrance of my son, Eamon, and my husband, Alec, who passed away April 24, 2022.

CONTENTS

ACKNOWLEDGMENTS

For the man on the street in Rosslare, Ireland, who inspired me to write this Holocaust novel about a Jewish ghetto in Dublin, Ireland, causing Nazis to bomb neutral Eire. Although I have not proven a ghetto existed in Dublin, I found areas in Dublin where Jewish families lived, and Jewish businesses thrived there for generations.

Thank you to Jean O'Connor, English department colleague and friend, as publisher of Mountain Pine Publishing, for formatting my newest novel, *Eyes Everywhere: Searching for Jewish Children*, designing the cover, and the photographs of Jewish artifacts.

I thank my cousin, Mary Jane Page Hellebust, who holds her English degree from Gonzaga, Spokane, Washington, for her careful first edit and suggestions.

Thank you to the Butte Archives for permission to share my photographs taken at the "Exhibition of the Jewish People" in Butte, Montana, in 2019.

Thank you to Dr. Beverly Chin for the invitation to share this writing adventure with her University of Montana Holocaust class. It was an evening I will forever remember with fondness. I had never spoken to a university class prior to this event. Her curious students about characters' outcomes were delightful, and one student, a close friend to a Jewish woman, added some details.

My Power Point presentation for Dr. Beverly Chin's class included photographs from newspapers and book excerpts. When I came home, my son, Eamon, said he was so proud of me. Eamon was stricken with Multiple Sclerosis two weeks after graduating from Carroll College in Helena, Montana.

Thank you to my daughter, Lucy, and her husband, Nate Lockwood, grandson, Gus, granddaughter, Elsie, and my Maine granddaughters Elise and Aubrey. Also, *Eyes Everywhere: Searching for Jewish Children* is written in remembrance of my son, Eamon, and my husband, Alec, who passed away April 24, 2022.

CHAPTER 1

Whispers Late at Night

Mother's and Father's whispers make my hands shake as I use chalk to draw under my bedspread. They think Minna and I are both in a deep sleep by now, but Grandfather gave me a flashlight that I reach for any night when nightmares begin. My nightmare is in a country I don't recognize where there are huge castles and brilliant green trees and climbing ivy, and I'm there alone with my six-year-old sister, Minna. Our parents aren't with us. Now, I'm awake and struggling to hear every word.

When Germany broke through the Polish border with their blitzkrieg, sending bombers through the air, Britain and France declared war on Germany on September 3, 1939. Mother begins to pack our clothes in August. She doesn't know that I opened my old suitcase looking for my favorite sweater last fall for the Roshashanah fishing trip with Father and saw her best sweaters.

Our radio in the living room announced that Nazis hit the village of Mokra near the border of Poland on September 1, 1939, and for the past two days, I hear Mother and Father tell secrets in front of Minna and try to trick her with codes.

We must be leaving soon, I guess, after I hear Father tell Mother he is purchasing rail tickets very soon. They quietly kiss and say goodnight and the kitchen light clicks off. The next few days are hard, pretending everything is normal with school, and breakfast, and dinner, and reading before lights-out time for Minna and me.

I am having nightmares almost every night. We are Jews. Our family worships in our synagogue, and soon I will celebrate my bar mitzvah when I turn thirteen. Preparations are underway with time spent studying the Talmud. Father says this is different than the Torah because the Torah is factual; however, the Talmud considers situations where the law is not definite. These are my last thoughts as I finally feel drowsy enough to sleep.

At school, my best friend, Richard, pulls out a charcoal drawing of the Warsaw Zoo's three silver foxes bred by the zookeeper, Jan Zabinski. Jan's wife, Antonina, welcomes artists whose paintings and drawings encourage financial support to increase the number of exotic animals. Mr. Bartels requires us to go to the zoo to select one animal to sketch.

Always I yearn to draw as soon as Mr. Bartels tells us our weekly assignment, but I haven't decided on which animal to draw. We've been in class all period, and I have not yet begun to draw. Richard is not a Jew, but a Catholic, so his family is probably not trying to escape. This is a difficult time for teachers and students.

Cover of a Babylonian Talmud, 1864

CHAPTER 2

⊂⊃ ∘◇∘ ⊂⊃

8 September 1939: It Started!

Father barges through the front door of the house yelling, "We have fifteen minutes before the soldiers arrive!"

"Has it started?" Mother calls.

"Mrs. Bartos is running down the street knocking on doors to warn Polish Jews that Nazis from a mile away forced Jews out of their homes. Some Jews are being rounded up in the street. The Warsaw Zoo has been bombed! I wonder if any of our favorite animals survived. Chaos everywhere! I ran for two blocks. Pack only essentials."

Mother doesn't even call Father by his name, Saul, when she asks "Has it started?" She pulls Minna's long-abandoned black baby carriage from the hall closet, and fills the bottom with the finest jewels and the silver menorah from Bubbe. I wonder when she selected these as she wraps jewel after jewel in the soft bath towels. *When had she and Father decided we might leave immediately?*

"Peter, could you go into Minna's closet and bring down the brown suitcase?"

"Don't you want Bubbe's tan leather bag? It's bigger."

"No, we don't want a leather bag. We want only the plainest suitcase."

"Why is this suitcase so heavy, Mother?"

"Minna's, Father's, and my clothes are packed in it. You have been growing so quickly, Peter, I didn't know what size you might be when we left. I want you to add three pairs of your socks, three pants, four shirts, three sets of underwear, and your two warmest sweaters.

"Saul, there is a jar of peach jam on the top shelf in the pantry," Mother continues. "Two loaves of fresh bread are on the stove. Please wrap two towels around the bread, since it is still hot from the oven. Also, please take the two cardboard boxes of food from the left bottom cupboard."

I stand holding the heavy suitcase because I don't know what to do next.

"Minna, please bring your favorite doll and your favorite book," Mother says.

"Chana, I'll bring our savings with us!" shouts Father as he opens the top dresser drawer in their bedroom.

"We need our winter coats," says Mother, as Father moves light coats aside and folds winter coats into a valise.

Minna stands with her eyes wide, her words lost. Mother, Father, and I scurry.

Father lifts the heavy baby carriage onto the sidewalk, and then paces, impatient for us to hurry.

I glance around our bread-fragrant kitchen, into the tidy living room, and then hold the door open for Mother and Minna. Father stops his pacing and we set the suitcase on the bottom rack of Minna's baby carriage.

The bombing by the Luftwaffe on September 1, 1939, signaled the serious threat to Warsaw. *Is that when Mother began to pack the suitcase and selected the jewels for our escape?* September 1, 1939, in Poland, would not be a date I would forget. Now September 8, 1939, will be etched in my mind forever as our lives change, when Nazis storm into Warsaw.

Mother lifts Minna into the baby carriage as Minna struggles to break free.

"I'm not a baby!" she screams, but Mother quickly covers her mouth.

Minna remains silent, almost frozen, as Mother wheels the baby carriage frantically out the door.

We walk quickly, almost running out of the city toward the forest, because rumors, hissed words in the air, tell of people being shot randomly in the street. A woman running alongside me says, "Nazi soldiers held a Jewish man's arms and laughed as one of the soldiers thrust a pair of scissors at the old Jewish man and mimed directions for him to chop off his beard. That old man looked afraid of cutting himself, and was so humiliated and sad."

I stop and remember my drawings in my leather-bound portfolio at school, but it is now too late.

"*Piotr*, you need to keep up with us," warns Father.

Father never calls me by the Jewish *Piotr* instead of Peter. He is shaken.

I thought of my best friend at school: Richard. He didn't face anti-Semitism, since he is a Catholic. *Will he be shocked when I don't show up for school? Maybe he will keep my portfolio for me, so I can get it when we return.*

"We'll be back soon. I believe this terror will soon pass," Mother whispers to me, as Minna whimpers quietly in the baby carriage.

Mother hums to quiet Minna, while we race toward the forest. I am happy the baby carriage has a hood-like cover, so Minna can't see the throng of hysterical people. My eyes widen as more and more frantic people move like a herd of scattered sheep. Not like cattle that seem to form lines. This is an unplanned exodus from home and country.

Old people after a short distance drop bundles of remembrances and some necessities to allow them to trudge on. Mothers and fathers hold tightly onto the small fingers of three-year-olds and they cradle babies. The September sun is relentless on our faces. Our family didn't spend hours out-of-doors and I know my chin is scorched.

Father is usually optimistic, but today he is grim. Muttering, it's like he's memorizing a list of names and addresses under his breath. As Father loses track of his mumblings, I can tell this list is alphabetized.

After we're deep in the dense forest, I lean closer and brush my face against Father's black beard. I whisper, "Whose names are those?"

Father says, "Don't worry, Peter, but from now until we are safe, I can't tell you or your mother anything, for your sake. Minna might hear us and being such a chatterer, she could endanger many people."

We find shelter near a willow tree. The huge gnarled tree trunk calls to my hands to use my piece of charcoal (always in my pocket) to draw all of the crevices and years of weathered wood. The swoosh of the green ground-touching branches sounds like a lullaby while dim light fades to a starless sky.

"I don't want to eat," Minna says, but she licks peach jam from the edges of her bread and then eats the crust.

We eat the bread spread with Mother's golden peach jam, and drink the tea from the thermos. Then we all stretch on the ground and fall asleep. After one more day of walking further into the forest, we backtrack to board the Nord Express, Calais from Warsaw to Paris, to stay with our grandparents.

Cars on the train are full but no one stands in the aisles. The strong acrid fumes of the stalled engine compete with the hunger I feel. Father unfolds sheets of art paper and hands them to me. The charcoal from my pocket is in my fingers quickly as I draw the compartment. I sketch Minna's drooping profile with her thick curly black hair drawn back from her face. *I wish her hair weren't so black. I wish Mother had blue eyes. Why was my hair blond? Why did I have blue eyes?* Next, I draw Father's and Mother's hands: They wear identical gold wedding bands with three delicate scrolls. Nobody would guess that these simple but lovely bands are worn by the finest Warsaw jeweler and his wife.

As Father frequently comments, "Only those knowledgeable know the highest quality of gold when they see it."

A porter leads us to a dining car where Minna asks for a lemon phosphate.

"Mm." Minna enjoys the first sip more loudly than we are allowed at home.

Father orders pot roast for all of us. We savor the tender meat and the sweet carrots in salty gravy.

Mother laughs at something Father says and leans back in her chair. She's sat stiffly for so many months. I love remembering her frequent laugh at the dinner table in Warsaw. I begin to sketch the boots of a young Nazi soldier not much older than I, six rows away. *I wonder where he is going.*

"I miss my violin lessons with the other students," says Minna.

Mother says, "Just hold an imaginary violin, Minna. Be like the mime at the Bar Mitzvah last year." She turns to face Minna and speaks softly, "I sent Bubbe your violin last month."

"How did you do that? No mail or packages came to our house for many months."

Mother smiles, "Remember, when I told you the best violin string could only be replaced by the finest violin shop?"

"Yes," whispers Minna.

"Now, you know, the finest violin shop happens to be next door to Bubbe and Grandfather's apartment."

Minna is quiet, a faint smile in the corners of her mouth.

Mother whispers to Minna, "Think for now, until we are back in our berth, try to play all of the notes of your favorite song with only your memory."

After our lunch, Father folds his white napkin and places it near his empty plate, we stand up and leave. We return to our berth. Mother and Father stretch to rest, but only one of them seems to close their eyes at a time.

Mother looks thinner. Always slender with dark brown curls, her dress hangs loosely. She looks neat, but never flashy. She often wears a locket with our pictures (Father's on one side, and Minna and me on the other side) around her neck. The gold chain and the gold locket with etched flowers are designed by Father.

Because I can't sleep, I continue my drawing, shading the sturdy soldier's boots where his ankle bends and remembering Mr. Bartels's lecture about the plight of the Gypsies in Poland. He told us of the Nazi uniforms and the loud sound of their boots on the road. *Why had Hitler suddenly ordered Gypsies to be sent to Buchenwald?*

"Why would Jews and Gypsies be a worry?" I must have said this aloud, because Father glances at me. He doesn't answer, but stares straight ahead.

Three days later the train stops near Remagen, Germany. Nazi soldiers come aboard and search passengers. Linens and jewels are taken. There's a poor family seated in the front compartment. We hear their voices and the older woman, probably a Jewish grandmother, screams that she needs her locket back. Soldiers yank it off her neck, as she sinks back into her seat.

Father says, "Let's return to our berth now."

When the soldiers knock on our door, immediately our father cautiously opens it. I slide the charcoal into my pocket and put my drawings into the seat pocket. Minna bites her lip like she does when she's scared. Mother clasps her hands in her lap to still her nerves.

Father unpacks the satchel with our clothes. The older soldier sees their matching rings, but the younger soldier scoffs at the similar plain bands and they leave.

I remember that Father assumed the jewelry business early when his father died. His father, my grandfather, opened the Knobel Jewelry Shop. Father was twenty, and Mother, an eighteen-year-old, when they married in their synagogue and exchanged those rings. I watch the boots of the soldiers, sounding harsh and heavy on the train floor, as the train car door closes.

Outside of the train, the sides of the luggage compartment raise and some crates and suitcases are opened and thrown to the ground. Clothing and books are strewn about, as the owners of the items scream out protests. Father lifts the corner of the shade on the window to see if Minna's baby carriage is pushed to the ground. When Father sees no baby carriage, he exhales slowly.

The train begins to chug and then roll free, and the sweat under father's nose evaporates. Quietly, our parents mouth prayers of thanksgiving.

The next day Mother and Father take sponge baths. I splash cold water on my face as well. It feels invigorating. Then Minna dresses in her favorite flowered dress to meet our grandparents in Paris.

So many days pass without fresh air and walks. I feel lonely without our neighborhood and synagogue. At times in Warsaw, I would wish we could go to movies more often. Now, I ache for the regular weeks, the well-ordered school, the almost monotonous recitation. We'll miss Rosh Hashanah and the fall celebration at the River Wislaw when Rabbis gather at the river to offer thanksgiving for the day and for the fresh fish for families.

A Menorah, a Many-Branched Hebrew Candelabrum

CHAPTER 3

With Our Grandparents in Paris

Screech! Chugs and squeals on the train tracks. On and on goes the travel, broken only by bits of sleep. Then, hot, intense fumes irritate my nose as the brakes of the train grab, and we suddenly stop. The Paris train depot is crowded, confusion on the faces of children, parents, and old stooped women, and men who move slowly without direction. Rigid soldiers with rifles slung over their arms watch those leaving and those who meet them.

Eyes are definitely now going to be the subject of my drawings: malice in soldiers' eyes, joy in Mother's eyes, relief in Father's eyes, and wonder in Minna's eyes as she gazes at the great number of people. Glancing at the sidewalk, we see Bubbe and Grandfather, who can't conceal their smiles.

Grandfather gently touches the collar of my coat and says, "Peter, it's good to see you." The taller of the two soldiers closest to us stares for a minute too long as

Grandfather's fingers drop off my collar. I want to tell the soldiers to move, but no one can tell a Nazi soldier, "Move."

Mother hugs Bubbe and quickly we open the doors to the taxicab that is waiting just before Mother's mask-like smile dissolves into tears. I look left, then right, for Grandfather's olive-green Citroen, his French automobile.

"I see you're looking for the car, Peter, but I don't want to attract attention by owning an automobile in front of these ever-present soldiers," whispered Grandfather.

Our luggage is set down from the train car and six of us crowd into the taxicab in the sweltering fall heat.

Grandfather chuckles, "You couldn't do without Minna's baby carriage, Chana? " as Father lifts the baby carriage into the boot of the taxi.

"You know how I love long walks. She can't walk as far as I," explains Mother in a louder than usual voice, because the shorter soldier nearly leans against the open window of our cab.

Grandfather asks Father, "Can you believe Paris has only 12,000 cabs, Saul?"

"How many were there when you came for banking business, Henri?" Grandfather and Father look surprised when they realize I am listening to them, but then continue their conversation.

"Back in the early 1930s, there were more than 20,000 cabs zipping around Paris. My banking transactions led me so often to Paris and I rode in those cabs."

"How often were you in France, Grandfather?" I ask.

Grandfather reveals more to me than I ever realized. "For a long time, I advised my clients and your parents to move their money out of Warsaw—away from Adolf Hitler and the anti-Jewish sentiment. Warsaw business people and wealthy Poles trusted me to care for their monies as my own money was being carefully protected."

As we drive along the 9th Arrondissement, I see many people in the street.

"Since Kristallnacht, I have not felt completely safe even here in Paris," Bubbe whispers to Mother. "One year of fear!"

"I felt safe since our family kept quiet in Warsaw—never a blemish on our family. I thought if we were quiet and didn't become involved in politics our lives would be safe," says Father to Grandfather.

Bubbe holds Minna's right hand and gently wipes away the wrinkles on Mother's forehead with her left hand.

Minna still hasn't spoken, but I notice her knees appear to knock against each other.

A group of four boys about my age pass around one cigarette on the corner of Boulevard St. Germain and Boulevard St. Michel. One boy looks like my best friend Richard. We'd never smoked cigarettes. I rub my thumb against my index finger not to cry as I think of Richard. There wasn't time to say goodbye to him or even to our neighbors.

In the cab, Mother says, "I will play a newly composed 'Violin Sonata in C Major' when we are home, Bubbe."

After we reach their apartment, we unpack. There are two bedrooms for our family. *Where will Minna and I sleep?*

Bubbe says, "We were afraid to rent enough space for both of the children to have separate rooms, Chana. So afraid you might not escape. Others watch us." She can't stop the one tear that trickles from her left eye. "There are *kopgeld* even here in Paris who receive a head price for turning in non-French Jews."

"What are *kopgeld,* Bubbe?" I ask.

"Spies."

Mother shakes her head in disbelief at neighbors turning against neighbor.

After the bags are put away, everyone wants to walk in the fresh air. Mother lifts Minna into the buggy.

"What're you doing? I'm too big for this!" Minna grits her teeth.

"You were quiet when we left Warsaw for the forest. Why are you now upset?"

"It seemed like an adventure, Mama."

"Doesn't today seem like an adventure?"

"No, it's like it's normal, I'll feel silly."

"What about just for today, Minna?" says Grandfather encouragingly.

"Well, if it's just for today," Minna snuggles into Grandfather's arms, as he picks her up and places her under the blanket, careful to cover her too long legs in the baby carriage.

"I'm still afraid." Mother moves closer between my grandparents.

"Have faith," Bubbe whispers.

Father and Grandfather walk ahead discussing something I can't hear because I am close to Bubbe and Mother.

Music on every corner. We don't heard jazz in Warsaw. Mother listens closely to the saxophone's sensuous sound.

Artists paint plein-air with containers for water on the sidewalk.

Mother leans closer to Bubbe. She forgets how closely behind them Minna and I follow. "Saul's business and the number of his customers kept dwindling. Politicians always came before Hanukkah to buy special jewelry; now businesses focus only on Jewish patrons. Instead of large jeweled designs, many Jewish husbands buy small jewels to be sewn into the hems or the seams of clothing. Now there is more caution even in gift giving for loved ones."

"I'm surprised since jewels are the first gifts for a wife as a bride and always the gift for Hanukkah," says Bubbe.

Back at our grandparents' apartment, while Father and I are alone, I ask, "When are we going home, Father?" I clear my throat. "I can't draw at night since Minna and I share the bedroom."

"Do you draw often at night?"

I hesitate. "My dreams are sometimes so strong I need to draw."

"What do you dream of, Peter?"

"My dreams are of a far-off place I know I've never been. It rains often. Everywhere I look there is too much green.

There are leaves and moss on rock walls. There are castles and people don't speak Polish."

For a few minutes, Father thinks, and accustomed to his thoughtful decisions, I wait. He looks mystified by my dreams. "You could set up a small studio for your drawing below the staircase in the kitchen."

"Yes!"

"I'll ask Grandfather if he doesn't agree this is a great idea. What would you need for your art studio?"

"A desk and a chair and a light. It would seem like drawing under my covers in my old bedroom when I was supposed to be asleep."

Two days later, I assemble charcoal, watercolors, and assorted weights of paper on the desk.

I am haunted by my dreams because Father and Mother are not there, only Minna and me, as we are now: young. In those dreams, people without faces are always adults. Even in sleep there is no one my age. The faceless people ignore me and Minna.

It is strange to be so haunted. Now, we're settled permanently in France with our grandparents.

So far, though, our lives seem temporary because we haven't been to synagogue with Father leading worship as he does at home. We aren't enrolled in school for next term, so Mother teaches us lessons.

Minna spends time with her violin and Mother instructs her. When the window in the dining room is open, people gather outside to listen to the confident notes. Minna is a gifted musician, especially for her age.

Grandfather only knows how lonely I feel.

"Did you know Toulouse Lautrec lived on Montmartre with many other artists, Peter? We'll go to see Monet's gardens. It's said that Monet 'painted the air' by rising before dawn and capturing colors in the light." We walk the boulevard of the artists. "Toulouse Lautrec and Monet found vision in Paris. I like the emotions in Lautrec's faces: he only portrays commoners in common settings, but the hidden emotions in the people's shaded eyes intrigue me," says Grandfather.

I almost forget how much I crave art. Seeing art in person is energizing, but it's also agonizing because my fingers yearn to feel the chalk, to remember the lines and the shadows. I miss art class. Richard loves the thickness of oil paint on the canvas, that smell of turpentine to clean the brushes, the dense scent of oil that lingers even over the weekend and assaults my nose when I enter the classroom on Monday morning.

As we walk down Montmartre Avenue, the *Biscuiterie de Montmartre's* beautiful confections lure us inside. A sign for Gateau St. Honre is set in the center of the window at 16 Rue Norvins. It looks like a tree of small creme puffs topped with crisp caramel drizzled wires. I follow Grandfather inside to order blackberry profiteroles, and we move outside as Grandfather sips his tiny cup of café.

"Do artists draw and paint with the world at war, Grandfather?"

"Pablo Picasso left Spain in the midst of war to move here to Paris. Isn't that ironic considering Paris is now threatened by Nazi control?" Grandfather asks.

I wonder what is he painting now. Does he only see refugees and Nazis? Can he continue his art?

When we return to the apartment, Mother and Father are arguing loudly as Father waves a letter.

"I need to return to quiet authorities' questions and to check on business," says Father. "The official asks why we have not returned from our visit to your parents. I'll tell them Grandfather is not well."

"I don't care about the business," Mother replies, trying to silence the fear I hear in her voice.

I know Father left only the lowliest jewels in the store.

"When will you leave?" I am mentally back in the present with its terrible reality.

"In two days, I should leave, so you, your mother, and Minna are safe."

Never before has Mother cried in front of us. Grandfather's face looks gray. His hand gently rests on Father's shoulder, and he leads Father away from Mother.

"Saul, I feel we must move Chana and the children to a neutral country soon," says Grandfather in a whisper, forgetting I am still standing close by them.

"Where is it safe?" Father stares out of the sheer panel on the window, not waiting for Grandfather's reply. Grandfather tips his head sideways twice to let Father know that I'm listening to their conversation.

"Are you certain you will again get out of Poland?" Grandfather's tears in his eyes show he does not worry that Minna and I are there.

"Of course," Father says in a quiet voice. "For another month everyone should be safe and by then I should return."

The morning at the train station is chilly and quiet. Everyone except Minna holds back tears.

"Father, please don't go. I won't be able to sleep if you aren't here."

"Oh, Minna, I wish we could all be back home, but if our business is safe, maybe we'll be able to return home."

Father hugs me so tightly I nearly cry. His face is so different without his beard. He thinks he will attract less attention without his beard, so his face is now smooth. Few men except Jews have beards in 1939.

"Take care of your sister!" Father pleads.

"Mother, Grandfather, and Bubbe will watch over all of us. Besides, you'll be back soon. One month is not long," I say, but I think of how many changes have come within one month, and so, one month will seem very long to Minna and me.

"Peter, take care." Father climbs up the stairs to the train. He doesn't wave to us, since soldiers watch all gestures.

Minna races up the stairs after Father, but I catch her on the second step and bring her back to Mother's arms.

CHAPTER 4

Jewish Children Tell of Escaping Nazis

Mother tries desperately to reach Father by telephone. Phone calls to our jewelry shop in Warsaw are answered by accents that are neither Polish nor French.

Mother asks, "May I speak to Saul Knobel?"

The voice says, "He is not in."

Finally, Bubbe's phone rings. Father is on the telephone. Mother holds the telephone receiver away from her ear so all of us can hear Father.

"As the train slowed to our boarding platform in Warsaw, Nazis randomly separate families. Ticket sales staff and the conductors wore German railway uniforms, and of course, spoke German. Destinations blared in German over loudspeakers. I decided not to get off the train immediately; instead, I moved to the baggage car, and found broken slats on built-in shelves. I hid under the slats in the dark."

Breathless, Mother asks, "Did anyone see you, Saul?"

"No. I don't think so. It was dark. After the railroad workers left, I moved from building to building until I reached our store. My key won't unlock the door. As I peered through the windows, I saw all of the jewelry cases were empty and the glass cases shattered. As soon as the faint light jarred me back to terror, I ran to the train station, and bribed the conductor to keep watch for Nazis soldiers while I journey toward Spain."

"Saul, I pray and worry about you every day."

"People will gladly take bribes, and jewelry is always better than coins. I was afraid I would be caught if I called you earlier, Chana. Even more than that, I was afraid you, Peter, and Minna would be forced to return to Poland."

"You would not recognize the store," he whispers.

"We're so happy to hear your voice," says Bubbe, as Saul's voice cuts away.

Mother stares at the phone and turns away from us. "We need to hurry and finish packing and then sleep well for a few nights, Peter and Minna."

Our grandparents' apartment in the evening is too quiet even for drawing.

In the mornings, violin lessons continue on Minna's repaired violin. Minna's fingers are stubby, but she plays every note so certainly that even strangers stop to listen.

Mother stares at the oil painting of a moonlight sailboat that is as dark as her eyes. She looks lost like she is when she hears beloved music.

"I left our Stradivarius copy in our home in Poland, hidden beneath one loose plank in our bedroom floor. That should be proof that we plan to return home. Shouldn't it?" Mother asks Bubbe.

Bubbe nods but her face looks troubled. Mother and I begin to quickly pack for what Bubbe tells her friends will be our return to Poland. Mother doesn't think the baby carriage will be a good hiding place this time. She takes only three jewels sewn into the hem of her heavier traveling dress. The other pieces of jewelry will be sent by Bubbe when we arrive.

Minna tells everyone, "We will see Papa."

Mother doesn't smile and her lips are tightly closed, so I know there is going to be a different journey—not back to Warsaw.

One week later at the Gare de Lyon train station, Bubbe cries softly as Minna kisses her goodbye. "I worry, when we will be together again?" Bubbe asks.

Grandfather whispers as he stares at his old man's hands. The veins are nearly outside of his thin skin. He leans in toward Mother. "We'll send jewels as you need them, sewn inside toys for the children, Chana. Gifts, of course, must be sent for traditional Christian holidays, not Jewish holidays even. . . ." His voice trails off since Minna is now listening.

This train station, all gold and crystal, was designed to stun World Fair attendees in 1900. All of the beauty is overshadowed with our raw feelings. Mother looks like a young child as her parents each take turns hugging her for the longest time. Bubbe breathes my hair for remembrance as she kisses my forehead. Minna laughs and jokes because she believes we will join Father in Warsaw.

A moonless night when we leave makes it difficult to even see each other's faces. I have my portfolio from my stay in Paris under my arm this time. Grandfather once had been a young artist, but he gave that up to become a banker, so his charcoal still can be used. He gives me several pieces, and buys new paper for our next destination in Spain. Since that was Father's last location, I feel certain Spain will be our next home.

Bubbe hugs Mother again for a very long time.

"I can't believe this persecution has not ended. I miss my synagogue and Poland," says Mother.

Mother looks like she is trying to memorize every smile line on Grandfather's face and then the eye smile lines on Bubbe's face.

Minna hugs the violin case that I'll carry to our seat.

"We'll call often," Minna promises Bubbe. "Our friends will be so happy to see us again."

Mother and I exchange glances that whisper, "Lies are not lies if life is saved."

The train chugs heavily, roaring to life, as we make our way down the aisle. There are so many large-eyed children and thin women in the seats on the train.

"These children's cheeks are hollow," says Mother, surprising herself as she hears herself saying aloud her thought. In an even louder voice, Mother says to me, "I wonder how long these children have been traveling from their homes, and then hiding until passports can be arranged."

When the train crosses into Spain, the Pyrenees come into view.

As Minna looks out the window, she asks, "What are those men throwing?"

"Spanish men run alongside the train, throwing single oranges from huge baskets to grasping fingers in open train windows," the young girl seated ahead of us explains to me. "They know how hungry all of us are on this train."

Those young Spaniards in white shirts racing alongside seem to be accustomed to this attempt to help the starving exodus. It's like a scene in a movie. Their aim so accurate and well-timed.

Minna sits in a corner with five other children playing with her dreidel. A boy my age sits in a corner and stares out the window.

"Do you want to play checkers?" I ask.

He stares at me and exaggerates words with his mouth and lips. "I can't speak. But I do read lips."

His sister says, "My name is Sophie and this is my brother, Aaron. He stopped speaking when our parents were sent away on a train."

Sophie unfolds the tale of how they were taken from their home in Minsk and marched toward a train. "There were Nazis everywhere. When parents began screaming as they were separated from children, Aaron grabbed my hand and pulled me close to him. As the voices of Nazis and screams intensified, Aaron backed up with me behind him. A large empty barrel stood thirty feet away. He lifted me and placed me in the barrel slowly, so there would be no noise, and then he jumped in.

"The trains were finally loaded, one with males and one with females. After that train left, an elderly bearded man came to the barrel and knocked. He hid us in his apartment until he bought us tickets for this train."

Sophie and I look at Mother sitting with other Jewish women. She is eager to speak her Polish. Women huddle close. Mother shares the lunch Bubbe packed, breaking the three cut-in-half-sandwiches into quarters. After seeing the children's sunken eyes, she doesn't take even a quarter of a sandwich.

At the first stop, one-half of the Jewish travelers get off the train. Soldiers are waiting to see if they are truly met by family members.

Sophie and Aaron stay with us. Five women depart with baskets of food. Four wagon carts assist those who need rides to the homes of their relatives.

"Those who aren't met will be taken to the camp," Sophie tells us.

Mother writes the names of three of the women she'd met only a few days before as possible future safe contacts for Jewish families. One curious contact is in Ireland.

"How long until we get off the train?" Minna asks. "I want to see Papa."

"A few more days," says Mother.

Our parents are always truthful with everyone including Minna and me, but now I can't be sure if adults tell the truth any more than their children.

Aaron smiles as I draw. He points to the charcoal faces of hunger on strangers' faces.

Sophie thanks me for sitting with him and trying to talk with him.

"You wouldn't guess it, but my brother was the best storyteller in school," says Sophie.

"What stories did he tell?" I ask.

"He loves to tell the story of David and Goliath."

As she talks, Aaron smiles, remembering the spellbound look on his friends' faces as he slowly delivers the final lines.

Portugal turns out to be the final stop for our train. Aaron and Sophie also get off the train. *Where will they go? Will we see them again in our race to escape the Nazis?*

I turn to see Mother stand up, then she gestures to me to shake Minna awake, and for us to follow her off the train.

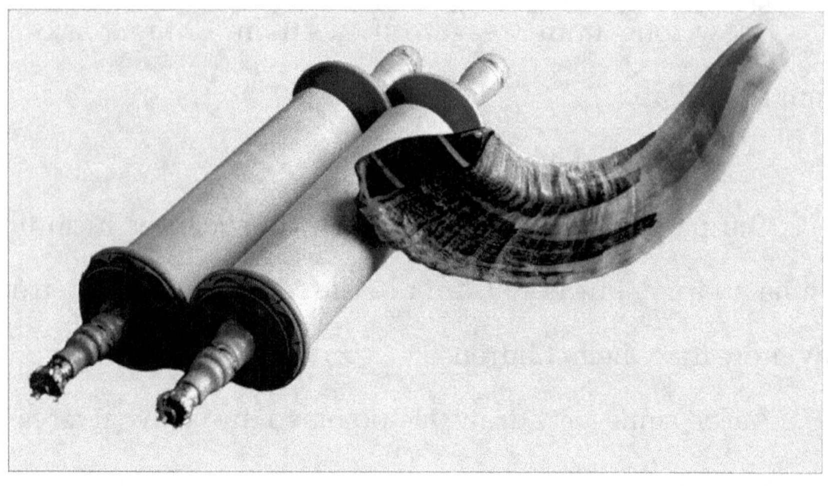

Shofar, *Ritual Musical Instrument Made from the Horn of a Ram or Other Animal, and Scroll*

CHAPTER 5

⬤ ◦ ◊ ◦ ⬤

"This is Not Warsaw"

"Why are we stopping here?" My eyes adjust to the tall buildings, then to the intense sunlight. *We are near water, from the scent in the air.*

"Where are we staying, Mother?" Minna wonders as she glances out the window. "Where is Papa? We aren't in Warsaw!"

"Your grandmother's childhood friend lives here. She's invited us to stay with her."

"You said we were going home, Mother." Minna looks as bewildered as she had when we left Warsaw.

I feel bewildered, too, but am old enough to know that this is not the time for questions.

A tiny bird-like woman waves.

"That has to be Dona Grace. She came to my parents' home many years ago," Mother says, wiping tears from the corners of her eyes at the sight of someone from her childhood.

"Chana, where is Saul?" asks Dona Grace as she sees just Minna and me with our mother.

Mother answers with a shrug and tears trickle down her cheeks. "We haven't heard from him for one month. Not since his call telling us that we'll join together in Spain. But he never arrived at the train depot. We used additional tickets to travel to Lisbon. Still, I didn't understand that he wouldn't be with us."

"You're all welcome to be here in Portugal." Minna is the first one Grace embraces, kissing her on both cheeks.

"Peter, Minna, in Portugal, you call female adults Dona and then their first name, so, this is Dona Grace."

"Chana, this is Antonio, my husband's old friend. Antonio, these are my dearest's friend's daughter and her children."

Dona Grace's driver takes our bags and Minna's violin case.

Seeing Minna's open-mouthed reaction to the colorful painted huge buildings lining the streets, Dona Grace explains, "Lisbon's buildings downtown were rebuilt after a huge earthquake in the 1800s."

On our drive, we see stucco buildings that are all painted in gentle pastel colors. Tall buildings form a protective pattern against the sky. Warsaw has no such colors on practical buildings. Even Paris did not feature colors as gentle as the sea.

"Pierre, my husband, died ten years ago." Dona Grace fingers the slender gold band still on her ring finger on the left hand, showing she still thinks of him often.

Mother asks Dona Grace about the flowers climbing up the stucco of the walls.

"Those brilliant pink bougainvillea vines look like exploded stars with the tiniest white center," replies Dona Grace.

The exterior of the house is painted turquoise. Inside, sheer gauze on the windows is so unlike our heavy drapes that keep out the Warsaw cold. The spacious home looks out on a beach. I long to take off my shoes and walk on the white sandy shore that we saw from her automobile. This tropical misty air feels soft and gentle on my face.

"I'm concerned that no further communication from Saul has come," Mother confides.

Dona Grace hugs Mother often and Mother looks relieved not to be the only adult making decisions. We go to the market to select fresh vegetables.

"We take so much for granted." Mother holds a ripe tomato as she looks at Minna and me.

Then, Dona Grace tells us, "You'll begin school again! The Jewish school is next to the ghetto where some immigrants are waiting to be deported. Sadness is on their faces as they hug their luggage and look longingly at the sea. They have been unable to get passports for Central America and will be returning to Poland."

I'm excited and Minna plans what she will wear for her first day of school. Teachers are Poles who left Poland long before even Kristallnacht, so their language is ours. I pack my art supplies, but on the first day, only rules are explained.

"No one must talk about their past life unless they want to," the young male teacher, Mr. Kemlawski, explains. Mr. Kemlawski fled Poland years before to study in Paris. When his school finished, Mr. Kemlawski's parents and sisters left Poland and now they all live together in Portugal.

"I won't try to tell any of you about the cruelty of the Nazis' regime," he tells us.

Mother and Dona Grace walk the short distance to school to accompany us home after our first day. The warm weather feels wonderful to me, but Mother misses cooler weather and the winter season at home in Warsaw.

I notice Mother wears her beautiful Polish scarf as a shawl. It's good to see the blue background with huge red poppies and roses. The tiny blue forget-me-nots on the shawl are more attention-getting than even the red poppies. Mother tries to hide her love of color since we left Poland. All of us dress in the drabbest clothes trying to blend into the sidewalks. I yearn to paint with such vibrant colors as I recall happier life in Warsaw in that scarf.

As we walk along this longer route home nearer the beach line, Mother and Grace talk about Bubbe's early years in Grasse, France. Minna and I trail behind them, so we still hear the conversation, but we aren't the center of attention for once. What a relief!

"Lisette was so much fun back then! We loved sitting at the cafés with our croissants and café, and we would watch young boys flirt with their girlfriends. We didn't have serious beaux then, and we loved working at the Bon Marché."

"Mother never told me she worked at a perfume counter."

"No wonder Bubbe always smells so beautiful," said Minna. I mentally sniff the sweet clean light flowery fragrance on my grandmother.

I'm surprised to think of Bubbe as a young woman. She always seems serious and worries all the time. Mother seems to forget Minna and I tag along with them as she is engrossed with this new portrait of her mother. *Does Mother know that Bubbe's name is Lisette?*

"I always heard that Bubbe and Father met in Paris. I never heard of her early years. Her parents had passed before I was born," says Mother.

"She was an orphan early in her life and lived in a children's home. I knew her from our early school years. My parents lived, but Lisette was strong, and quite beautiful like you, Chana. She loved supporting herself, but she also shared my family," smiles Dona Grace.

"We went to Lisette's father's family church, the twelfth century Cathedral Notre-Dame-de-Puy, for visits. Three large paintings by Rubens hang in the church. I believe Lisette loved the paintings maybe even more than religion. When we went to see the Rubens' paintings, we planned for an all-day trip."

"Wasn't Bubbe raised as a Jew?" asks Mother in a low voice so Minna does not hear the question, but I hear it. Minna is watching the shoreline to find seashells.

"No, many in Grasse were Catholics."

"Where is Grasse?" asks Mother.

"It's north of Cannes in the Southern Provence."

"Did you and Bubbe invent the fragrances?" I ask.

"Oh, no, Peter. We were not the '*nose.*' *Noses* are highly respected and much sought-after employees of great perfume houses. They blend the perfect scent."

"We worked at the Bon Marché's marble sales counters with customers," explains Dona Grace. "We answered questions from buyers from all over France and even other countries."

Mother asks Dona Grace, "Has perfume always been so expensive?"

"The answer begins with the number of flowers. Seven and one half million flowers produce only one kilogram of essential perfume oil," says Dona Grace.

"How are the flowers turned into perfume?" I ask.

"Women grab the blossoms and twist the calyx." Dona Grace demonstrates as she mimes twisting the calyx, from memory.

"Women lift their aprons to hold the flowers, while the *'videurs'* hold burlap sacks to collect flowers that must be taken to the factory in less than one hour before the fragrance changes," answers Dona Grace.

"How are the fragrances combined?" Mother asks. We become more and more curious about Bubbe's early career in the "parfum" industry.

"Copper stills in many shapes, such as cylinders and upside-down teardrop containers, are used, Peter."

"Grasse was known as 'the capital, *Mondiale des parfums*,'" continued Dona Grace.

"What does that mean?" Mother asked.

"It is translated as 'the world's perfume capital,'" says Dona Grace.

"When did Grasse become the capital of perfume?" asks Mother, fascinated by this detail about her mother's work in the perfume industry.

"Since the end of the 18th Century."

"What caused such an interest in Grasse?"

"There are roses, tuberose, mimosa, but especially jasmine, that set Grasse fragrance apart. Jasmine was brought to the south of France in the 1600s by the Moors."

"What did Grasse look like?" asks Mother. She cannot stop asking questions about Bubbe's early life in France.

"Oh, it was so beautiful, such narrow streets, such soft pastel orange buildings, and the freshest air. Strangely enough, perfume was important to the leather and glove merchants to mask the odor of the tannery. Women began to wear perfumed gloves. And this was the beginning of the perfume industry."

"We should turn back here, Chana. I am a little winded from our tour," said Dona Grace.

"I haven't even noticed your beautiful scenery here in Portugal because of all these exciting details from Mother's early life."

"For another day, Chana. I must reveal how your parents met and how I met my darling husband in France."

CHAPTER 6

Telegram: Our Mother Must Return Alone

The next day Minna and I walk a few feet ahead, as Dona Grace and Mother sip tea at an outdoor table and look over the Atlantic Ocean. The beaches are covered in the whitest sand. Minna and I search for the biggest sea shells. Almost immediately, Minna finds one large conch shell, so we move near Mother.

"It's so wonderful to let the children roam where I don't have to accompany them and worry every second," says Mother.

Then in a quieter tone, she asks, "Do you mind a question, Dona Grace?"

"No, dear, please do feel free to ask anything."

"Why is Portugal safe while other countries send even children to ghettos?"

"Portugal's neutrality is allowed to prevent Spain from joining the Axis powers. Spain appreciates the ports in Portugal keeping transportation flowing," replies Dona Grace.

"Where do refugees go when they leave Portugal?" asks Mother.

Dona Grace moved her wrought iron chair closer as she lowers her voice and she begins to share the political situation in Lisbon. "There have been more than fifteen hundred Jewish citizens who have come to Portugal. Salazar, the Fascist Spanish dictator, forbids the entry of Jewish and Russian refugees in Spain, but Portugal's diplomat, de Souza, allows Jews to remain here for thirty days."

I can hear them discussing this history of Lisbon and Portugal as neither wind nor waves guard their conversation.

Dona Grace continues explaining politics. "Our head of the government, Aristides de Sousa Mendes, chooses not to obey Salazar. De Sousa signs visas in Bordeaux, perhaps even your family's visas on to Paris. It's said he signed documents twenty-four hours a day."

"How're we allowed to enter Portugal through Spain?" asks Mother breathlessly.

"Your father, Chana, has many contacts. Your passport was secure to leave Paris, travel through Spain, and live here in Lisbon. If possible, then Jewish immigrants try to arrange transport to North America or South America from Lisbon," answers Dona Grace.

"Is there a closer route than North or South America to reach safety?" asks Mother as she moves closer to Dona Grace.

Dona Grace shakes her head, "No."

"Is there another neutral country besides Portugal?" asks Mother.

Dona Grace thinks for a minute. "There've been rumors of Jews living near Dublin, Ireland. Children are sometimes sent there by their families. Some children have also been sent to Northern Ireland; however, it's not as safe as is Eire."

"I thought Ireland fought with the Germans against Britain," says Mother.

"This war is expanding and now Ireland is divided with the Northern Ireland brigades supporting England. Southern Ireland is neutral, and technically, may not allow British boats to refuel in the South. Dublin is not pro-Germany; however, the old feud with Britain still is felt by many Irish people."

As Minna and I leave the shoreline, and move closer to them, Mother takes a shallow breath. "Can we talk about this later? I'm worried about Saul and all who flee persecution."

I startle to hear the fear in Mother's voice.

The next morning a telegram comes for Mother from Bubbe. "CHANA STOP YOUR FATHER IS GRAVELY ILL STOP SOLDIERS WATCHING STOP."

Mother looks like her mind is racing. "How can I reach Saul to let him know about Father's illness?" Mother asks Dona Grace. "We need to repack and leave as soon as possible for Paris."

Dona Grace shakes her head. "Lisette's statement about the soldiers means you shouldn't take the children with you. We sometimes talked in our own codes when unwanted suitors tried to ask for dates. When Saul reaches your parents' apartment, you and he will find your way back to Portugal. You'll need visas again. It must be soon because our leader, de Sousa Mendes, is facing terrible pressure to discontinue issuing visas."

"Has he been ordered to immediately limit or stop visas?" Mother asks in a strained voice.

"Not at this time; however, there is pressure by the Axis powers to limit exodus through Portugal. Refugees are only allowed to stay in Portugal for thirty days before they must leave for a new country or return to their native country."

"Dona Grace, will you keep Peter and Minna here on the pretext of completing their term? I know Peter and Minna want to see their grandfather, but it's not safe now."

"That's a reasonable response for anyone who asks, Chana. I will care for Peter and Minna as I would care for my own grandchildren, if I had grandchildren, until you return."

My face flushes with the terror I feel. *How can we live here in such a strange country with someone we just met?*

Mother turns to me. "Will you watch over and watch out for Minna? Will you promise to always care for her until we are all united?"

"I'll always take care of my sister," I say, but I gulp as I draw in too much air, so I won't say how terrified I feel to make such a promise.

Mother begins to pack a small suitcase, and then purchases the train ticket back to Paris.

When she returns from the train depot, Mother asks Dona Grace, "If I am stopped and questioned by a Nazi soldier, what reason do I have for returning to Paris from Portugal? If I say it is because of my father's health, neighbors may question why Saul and the children are not returning with me."

Dona Grace suggests, "You can say you were teaching a violin protege in Portugal, and now are returning to Paris to teach violin, while the children complete their school session. Then Saul and the children will return to Paris. You must avoid answering questions as much as possible," warns Dona Grace.

"Also, you need to color your hair to try to disguise yourself," Dona Grace worries about Mother's Jewish appearance. She looks Mother up and down.

"I've never wanted to have fair hair," says Mother. She slowly pushes back her dark hair from her face.

"What color will your hair be now, Mother?" asks Minna with a shocked look on her face.

"What color would you suggest, Minna? Peter? What color hair would be the best for me."

I will not be caught up in this frivolous mood. I say, "Only blond hair seems to be the preferred color now, Mother."

"I agree," says Dona Grace.

"Won't my dark eyes stand out even more?" Mother asks.

"I'll find smoked glasses for you. If asked you could say you have conjunctivitis," Dona Grace answers.

"Mother, what is conjunct...?" asks Minna, unable to recall that complete word.

"It's an eye infection that is treated with a salve, but it causes burning and itching and you should stay out of the sun." Mother adds, "Grace is very quick with believable stories, isn't she?"

Dona Grace may not have mixed the fragrances for perfume, but she can mix vegetable dyes to turn Mother's dark hair blond. She looks natural with her new hair, especially when she pulls on smoked glasses. She could almost be a German woman.

Mother's travel dress is one of Dona Grace's. Despite the age difference, Dona Grace is more fashionable than Mother. The navy-blue dress with a belt makes Mother look younger. Dona Grace gives her a camel hair wool coat, too, for the cooler weather in Paris.

"My husband was in the export tile trade for all of our life. Since I met and entertained his clients, my clothing reflected our status in society."

"What would Saul think of this dress?" Mother wonders aloud.

"He would love it, Mother," says Minna, touching the hem of the dress.

Mother leaves for the train by herself Sunday morning. She looks alone as she closes Dona Grace's front door slowly. Antonio will drive her to the train. I want to go with her, but even Dona Grace stays at home. Dona Grace doesn't want to attract any attention to Mother, leaving without her children.

Monday morning, Minna and I leave for school with a sack lunch. We know our destination well. Minna is in the *Jardim de Infância* (Kindergarten class), and I am in *Ensino Basic* (Basic Education for students through the seventh grade).

As we walk from school to Dona Grace's home, Minna tells me, "I love my first recess game. Two girls hold hands and run slowly in a circle of other students holding hands. The speed is then very fast when someone yells, 'Wheel! Wheel!'"

"That sounds very exciting, Minna," I say, as my mind flips back to our recess game in Warsaw. These are games like *"Serso,"* the toss and catch a ring on a stick played by two. Usually, I play this game with Richard after we eat our lunch and go outside for recess. We watch Marcelina and Alicja play "Glass Piece Secrets." They find a smooth piece of glass and small treasures that it will hide. Marcelina digs a small hole, and Alicja puts a flower in the hole. Then Alicja covered the glass and the secret with dirt.

I grow sad thinking about my classmates, wondering where they are, knowing we may never meet again. With Mother now gone as well as Father for more than one month at least, it is difficult to be cheerful even in a regular classroom. When Minna enters her classroom, she smiles and that lifts my dark feelings for a minute.

CHAPTER 7

New Traditions for Our Sabbath

Dona Grace's life in Portugal is much more social than Bubbe's life in France. Friends often send her invitations for lunch or dinner, but she stays home with us, and acts content to be there. Dona Grace tells me she always wished to be a mother and a grandmother like Bubbe is.

Dona Grace tells me, "We went out so often when Pierre was in his exporting business that I still enjoy just being home. Now, with you and Minna here, it is especially wonderful to have this home full of excitement."

Nazis are not living amongst us. Bombs are not falling. Jews are not being shot nor are they rounded up. Dona Grace's housekeeper, Rosanna, sets out breakfast on a sideboard in the dining room for us, as Dona Grace writes notes to her friends. She'll take us with her to post the letters tomorrow morning. No school on weekends leaves such a large chunk of time for us, but leisurely breakfast is enjoyable with Rosanna's delicious baking.

"Peter, do you like the *broa*?"

"Is this the *broa*?" I point to bread with a thick crust, and then savor a bite. "This is delicious. I think it's corn bread, isn't it? The strawberry jam is sweet."

"We don't have fruit every day at home," Minna says. She looks lost and sad this morning, but still enjoys the slice of orange, the sweet juice dripping on her chin.

"Rosanna, I would enjoy a *mega de elite*." As Grace turns to Minna and me, she says, "That is Portuguese for a cappuccino. Do you both enjoy your hot chocolate? Children and adults nearly always enjoy a hot drink for breakfast."

"We both love hot chocolate," Minna tells Dona Grace. Her tongue catches a drop near the corner of her mouth.

Minna smiles and tells Dona Grace about Warsaw breakfast. "Our old breakfast was most often almost always hot cereal, *kasza*, with a little brown sugar. Apples or plums are usually the only fruits in Warsaw. You have so many different fruits and vegetables!"

"Do you enjoy the dried salted sardines that Rosanna packs in your lunch?" asks Dona Grace.

"They're different than the little pierogis Mother made us," interrupts Minna.

"What are pierogis?" Dona Grace asks.

"They're like a small bundle of chicken and onions in a rolled pastry," I remember, almost tasting the flavors in my watering mouth.

I don't want to hurt Rosanna's, nor Dona Grace's feelings, but I haven't acquired a taste for the sardines yet.

Rosanna brings the cappuccino in a China cup with blue flowers. The saucer is as delicate as the cup.

"Since today is Saturday, what would you like to do?" Dona Grace asks.

"Usually, we go to synagogue on Sabbath," I answer. "On Friday night we read a book from our library. The remainder of Saturday afternoon we spend reading books from our school library."

"We'll look into this then," Dona Grace says. "Where is your synagogue in Warsaw?"

"On Tlomackie Street in Warsaw. It is, no, it was the biggest synagogue in the world when it was built, a wooden synagogue. Bubbe told us it burned during the bombing of Warsaw."

"Did Lisette, sorry, Bubbe, and your family go to the synagogue in Paris?"

"No. Grandfather knew how closely everyone was watched. Even though French Jews are not targeted, Grandfather didn't think it would be wise. We'd not been to France for a visit with Bubbe and Grandfather since they left for Paris two years ago. Deliberately, Grandfather made certain neighbors saw us walking about in Paris last month on Friday evenings and going to the market for fruit on Saturday."

"What should a fervent Jew do on Friday?" asks Dona Grace.

"Under Jewish religious law, *halakha*, Sabbath, begins just before sunset on Friday night, and Shabbat is observed Saturday night until three stars appear in the sky. Then candles are lit and prayers, and a blessing, is given. Bubbe loves bringing out the best candlesticks and the best linens for the dinner and the silver goblets for the wine," I say, seeing the candlelit dinner in memory.

"Is this celebration private—only for your family?"

"It may be private, but other Jewish members meet in the synagogue usually on Saturday morning. Some Jews celebrate in synagogue on Friday night. There is the *challah*, the special bread, to symbolize peace. It's a quiet time. Men wear the yarmulke on their heads."

"Your grandmother must have loved the celebration with all of you when you lived near each other in Warsaw."

We stay indoors and I try to recall stories from the Torah. Minna likes the quiet of Sabbath and doesn't need a reminder of our tradition on the weekend.

For dinner, Rosanna sets out the most beautiful blue and white ceramic candlesticks that look like Portuguese tiles.

"*Cozida a 'portuguesa,'*" Rosanna announces as the stew with chicken and vegetables is placed in the center of the table. It smells delicious.

Dona Grace mentions that Portuguese often make the stew with pork; however, she will not make it that way for our dinner. She is respectful of our tradition and that ingredient is not added. The dessert, *arroz done*, a rice pudding flavored with cinnamon, is a wonderful dessert for this Sabbath dinner.

After dinner we sit on chairs on the patio and watch boats return to shore. Minna hums a soft tune to herself. Sometimes, she makes up songs, and sometimes she hums violin scores that I recognize. Eventually, her head drops and I pick her up and carry her to her bedroom. She doesn't even awaken when Rosanna takes her sweater off, one arm at a time.

"Thank you, Dona Grace, for this memorable Sabbath. It's been a long time since we celebrated Sabbath."

"I'm enjoying my chance to be a grandmother to my best friend's grandchildren, Peter!" Dona Grace's eyes actually twinkle while she tells me not to worry about changes in our life with her in her home in Lisbon.

Torah *with Ornate Covering Featuring the Star of David*

CHAPTER 8

Bubbe Sends a Letter in Code

The next night, her door knocker clanks and a courier hands a telegram to Dona Grace. Telegrams now bring startling messages. Without waiting, she reads the telegram, and then she lifts her head up to tell me to follow her into the drawing room. Dona Grace appears startled, her eyes wide, and she bites the inside of her mouth.

In the drawing room, striped gold and cream wallpaper doesn't distract from six paintings of different seashells found on the beaches near Lisbon. My favorite is a cream and pink colored conch shell on a beach. Like Dona Grace, this room is calm and gentle. I hope the news might be calm, but I am sure that will not be the case. Dona Grace fingers the outline of the envelope slowly and then she gently opens the telegram. "From Paris," she says.

Minna's still upstairs with Rosanna, choosing her dress for tomorrow. Rosanna isn't only a cook; now she is like a governess to Minna. At first, they communicate with gestures. Sometimes, Minna spreads her arms wide and shrugs her shoulders to indicate she doesn't understand. Minna tries to speak Portuguese instead of gesturing to Rosanna.

I hear Minna say, "*Nom dia!*"

Rosanna responds, "*Como está?*"

Minna understands the question, "How are you?" but her answer comes out "No."

The sound of hangers slips across the closet rack indicating it will be some time before Minna smiles and points to her choice of a favorite dress.

Dona Grace opens the telegram. "I believe you have a right to know all news from your family, Peter. Although you are young, these times don't allow secrets in families. Shall I read the telegram aloud?"

I look at the floor and hold my right wrist with my left hand as I say, "Please do, Dona Grace."

Dona Grace reads, "CHILLY HERE STOP SO MISS HENRI` STOP SAUL NO TIME FOR US STOP."

Bubbe wrote the message, but I know, Mother sits next to her, as it is strange, like a code. But Dona Grace seems to understand her old friend's blank statements between words.

"What do you think she's saying, Peter?" asks Dona Grace. She looks directly into my eyes.

"I believe my grandfather passed away. When Bubbe says she 'SO MISS HENRI,' that is the only possible meaning." *It was such a short time ago that Grandfather shared his love of art with me. He was happy to set up the stairwell studio.* My mouth is suddenly dry.

"Bubbe is trying to warn all of us. French postmen bring mail; however, postal uniformed Germans are very much in charge and letters may be opened by the wrong hands, so telegrams must be carefully written," I reply.

"I don't want to believe it, but I agree that must be Lisette's hint to us," says Dona Grace.

"When Bubbe writes that father has not found time for them, I don't think he has yet contacted Mother. Where might he be?"

"Germans are closing borders more quickly than any of us thought possible. I'm sorry to tell you such terrible news. I can't even guess where Saul is hiding, Peter."

"How will we explain all of this to Minna?"

"Let's keep this telegram to ourselves for now. I want nothing more than for your lives to be happier. Changing the subject, I would like to find a violinist to expand Minna's skill on the violin. Your Mother must still expect me to offer violin lessons for Minna. Our music, *'fado,'* translates as 'fate.' It's melancholic, but also unusual. The *fado* guitar should be able to capture that mood. It's passionate, so it is not measured, boring music, suitable for someone as lively as Minna."

I hesitated. "Did Mother allow monies for our care?"

"Ah, yes, Peter, but none has been needed at this time. Chana left money and some jewels to be used if needed for you and Minna. Feel free to enjoy your time in Lisbon away from the frantic terror of Nazis. And what for you? Would you like art lessons?"

A bolder person than I would ask Dona Grace for a space to set up his art. It feels so temporary in this precisely perfect home, where there is a place for everything and everything in its place. The scent of chalk would even seem disruptive in the sea-scented house. A chalk scent would compete even with Bubbe's fragrance.

"My friend, Richard, from Warsaw and I both love art, but now my focus is gone, Dona Grace. News is sad, and it's difficult to know if news is true."

"What you need is a new glimpse of Lisbon. What would you say if Antonio, my driver and gardener, took you and his grandson to watch a *Touradas,* a Portuguese Bull Fight? This is

Antonio's idea, but you certainly don't have to accept the invitation."

"Thank you, but I don't think I would like the bloodshed of the bull."

"The bull fights in Portugal are different than Spanish bull fights. The bull is not killed in the arena, but challenged by a group of eight men who taunt the bull to charge."

"We studied Spain in our geography class. The sport of bull fighting seems brutal. Have you seen a bull fight, Dona Grace?"

"I only went to the bull fight once, Peter. The interchange between the rider on the Lusitano-bred horse and the wild bull is somewhat frantic, but I thought you'd appreciate the colors of the costumes and the flags! I so long for you to again find your art."

"Does the team dress like the Spanish bull fighters?"

"I'll wait until you have been to the bull fight to discuss the pageantry. I wouldn't suggest you go unless I thought this scene might compel you to pick up your art again. The colors of clothing on the rider and the horse are stunning. The interaction among horse, bull, and rider is so intense."

"Dona Grace, thank you. Could I think about going to the bull fight for a day?"

I know Dona Grace yearns to be a mother and a grandmother. I wish I could hug her to make her feel more like our grandmother.

Minna comes into the drawing room with her black hair braided, wearing a brown skirt and a blue and white checked blouse. Her shoes are scuffed from our walks on the beach. I need to ask Dona Grace for polish. Mother wouldn't approve of our scuffed shoes.

"Minna, I've mentioned to Peter that I want you to begin violin lessons here in Lisbon."

"Oh, no. When I pick up my violin, I miss home and Mother and Father."

"If you tried a new style of music, would that be fun?"

"What kind of music is played here?" Minna asks, a curious look in her eyes.

"It's very lively! Our music, *fado*, is for youth! Not so serious."

"I'll try!"

"I'll send a note to my friend, Vashti, who knows the best *fado`* guitar instructor in Lisbon."

"Thank you!" Minna smiles from her heart with a wide grin. It's good to see her happy.

Perhaps, I should see the Portuguese Bull Fight with Antonio. If Minna appears to need her music again, I, too, might begin to crave my art again.

CHAPTER 9

"Ah, Touro!"

From morning into afternoon on Sunday, I envision the *touradas*. My ears hear the roar of an excited crowd jeering at a bull and cheering on the bull fighter. My eyes see only red blood.

Rosanna answers the door when Antonio raises and then lowers the door knocker.

"I'm eager for you to share details when you return, Peter. Bull fights are only held from March through October. You are here for the last bull fight," smiles Dona Grace. Antonio stands nearby waiting for me.

"My grandson, Silvano, is your age. He waits in Dona Grace's car," says Antonio.

I am not sure how to anticipate this event. Our family life in Warsaw is quiet and animals are not taunted for fun. *How will I react?*

Antonio leaves Dona Grace's car in the parking area. We climb onto the yellow trolley. It moves too quickly, so even with huge windows the scenery passes too fast to notice details. As we approach Camp Pequeno, I see swirled Moorish turrets. Gates are open for the crowd. No one pushes, but the excitement is felt by straight-backed men and chatting women, anxious to find their seats. I'm surprised to see not everyone moves to their proper seat.

Tickets are printed with seat numbers, but if a man or woman is too tall in front of them, people can choose their favorite seat. Some older people count the seat numbers from the aisles. They yell if someone is in their seat, but the guilty ones don't leave and shake their fists to keep their seats from intruders.

A photo on the wall shows a rider in ivory lace and metallic gold. The men who try to bring down the bull by his horns wear dark everyday pants, red shirts, and small patterned scarves tied around their necks.

If I paint the scenes, I could add titles on the signage. I can't believe the vibrant colors! As we enter the coliseum, bright claret red and emerald green flags fly above the ring. A banner, "Portugal," in burgundy red letters on an olive banner stands in front of the entrance for the bull. One man dressed in a white shirt holds a gold flag.

Antonio points to a flag of Portugal, not the simple green/white/red stripe I see more often, but a flag with a red top and green bottom half showing the emblem for Portugal with the Portuguese shield outlined by a golden sphere.

"Our flag is symbolic with red symbolizing blood, the green is for hope, and those blue shields stand for five Moorish Kings who were defeated by our first Portuguese King," Antonio boasts.

I remember our Polish flag is crimson and white with crowned eagles in the center. Our flag is more fearsome than this Portuguese flag.

As the men enter the arena, crowds cheer for the men. Antonio nudges Silvano, who yells, "Olé!"

Then Antonio says, "Avatar," as he points to the men, waving with an expansive sweeping gesture to indicate all eight are a team.

Antonio and Silvano don't talk to each other as the challenge begins. Noise and dust rise when the bull begins to realize he's outnumbered and surrounded.

"*Olé, Caveleiro!*" shouts Silvano. A champagne-colored horse prances into the arena, its braided white mane elegant down its back. The *Caveleiro* wears gold and lace and holds a stake-like blue and white object. My mind quickly flashes to the day with Grandfather on Montmartre, and the blurred movement in Toulouse Lautrec's circus horses that we saw on a print in *Biscuiterie de Montmartre* when we ate the blackberry pastries. Powerful muscles and such strength reside in the flanks of the horses.

All of the frantic sounds in the coliseum mimic those first Nazi planes buzzing through the sky like mad dogs. Smells of burning wood wafted for days over Warsaw. I thought I could smell and taste blood even in the forest after we ran from Warsaw. Then I look at the bull and wonder. *Will the bull bleed tonight?*

As the bull charges the horse, the *Caveleiro* stabs the back of the bull. The bull reacts by leaping into the air. His snort is loud and echoes in the coliseum. One little girl in front of me stifles a cry. "Ah, *touro!*"

The movement of the horse interests me more than the dodging movements of the poor bull. The horse shifts quickly to avoid the horns of the bull. Silvano leans over and tells me, "The bull's horns are filed down and leather cups prevent the horse from being gored."

The bull doesn't like the screams of "Avatar!" "*Morre Touro!*"

I dislike hearing the creature bawling in pain.

Once again, Silvano, yells, "*Olé!*"

I hear myself yelling, "*Olé!*" as the second javelin pierces the bull. I cover my mouth with my hands. *How can I cheer against the bull?* With the third javelin, the dust under the bull's hooves lingers in the twilight air like sparkles on the Christmas tree in Warsaw square, but the bull shakes his massive head as though he can't believe he is in the arena. He stomps left, then lurches forward. I still can't believe I cheered against the bull.

The Avatar lurches at the bull's horns to take him down. I do not think eight to one seems fair, but the bull fights hard against being outnumbered. Even the capped horns can't cover the frightened yet fierce red and yellow color of the bull's eyes, shifting from one man to the next.

Young boys hold up pastries for the crowd. Silvano waves to a boy selling cups of beer and pastries. Antonio raises his right wrist toward me to see if I, too, will enjoy this fried food.

I smile and take a warm sweet-smelling pastry. The treat is so flaky it crumbles in thin strips. Almond paste and sliced almonds are subtle in flavor, but so sweet. Antonio reaches for a beer and hands the seller an *escudo*.

The crowd waves white napkins to confuse the bull. The general frantic excitement doesn't thrill me. I feel scared for this targeted animal. His downcast eyes bring to mind the older peoples' fleeing Warsaw alongside my family.

After the bull is thoroughly enraged, four pointy javelins in his back, the rider pulls on the bull's horns and the rider and the bull lock eyes. Then the rider bows to the crowd, and the bull with his eyes on the ground is led away.

Was this the end of the bull? Will the bull who loses this encounter be later killed as was the case for bulls in Spanish fights? Or will the bull, as Dona Grace said to me, be allowed to live his long life in a pasture? My heart aches for the vanquished *touro*.

Antonio waits until Silvano and I climb onto the trolley. Then he chooses a seat in a row three ahead of us to give us time to talk about the *tourados*.

CHAPTER 10

Another Telegram: Bubbe is Coming

My painting of my favorite Warsaw gathering captures our family around a Hanukkah dinner table. This is the happiest memory. Minna's just a one-year-old with potatoes in her hair. She squeals with laughter. Our grandparents still live in Warsaw. The world is not at war. Mother glows as she places *challah* on the table. Bubbe's silver candlesticks hold white candles. Father and Grandfather wear the *kippahs*, and I sit next to Minna.

My paintbrush holds a light gold blob of oil paint to shadow the candle flames. When the doorbell rings, my paintbrush drops to the floor and paint splatters. Hurriedly, I clean up the droplets with the cloth towel. Rosanna walks noiselessly as she always does, making the wait even more tense. Rosanna turns from the door to hand a telegram to Dona Grace, who sits on the love seat in the drawing room.

A nod of Dona Grace's head toward the drawing room brings me to the love seat. She pats the cushion to draw me nearer to her.

"Come here, Peter." Dona Grace pats the seat near her. She says in a soft tone, "I'm pleased to see that the bull fight inspires your art again. I'm sorry to interrupt your work."

Dona Grace opens the telegram and asks if she should read. I nod up and down. She reads, "EERILY QUIET STOP HENRI PEACEFUL STOP SEE YOU NEXT MONTH STOP."

This does not follow Mother's pattern of speaking, nor is there a clear message. Minna's fingers and bow quietly play her violin in the living room. Brahms's Hungarian notes lack Mother's part on the piano. *Minna will be upset to know that Mother will not join us soon. And Father's not even mentioned.*

"Isn't that great news that your grandmother is coming to you, Peter?" Dona Grace's mouth smiles, but her eyes do not.

"Yes, but I miss Mother and Father. I want all of our family to be together. It's taking much longer than Father planned." I hesitate, then look to the floor and ask, "Why did Mother sign such a contract, Dona Grace? For one more semester?" I try not to chew on the uneven finger nail on my left hand.

Dona Grace reaches over and places her warm, wrinkled hand over mine. "There must be great surveillance by spies for the Nazis in Paris. I'm sure your mother is afraid for both your father and for herself."

"Another semester will make it impossible for her to get out, won't it?"

"Let's not get ahead of ourselves, Peter. I don't believe she plans to finish the semester. She is waiting to see where she will meet up with your father."

"Wouldn't it be wiser for them to travel separately to Lisbon?" I ask.

"Chana must be protecting your father. He must be in greater danger than she," says Dona Grace with tears in her eyes.

There is silence as my mind focuses on Bubbe's journey to Lisbon. "How's Bubbe allowed to purchase a ticket to Lisbon?"

"Visits to Lisbon are allowed even for Parisian Jews now, Peter. For thirty days, in Lisbon. Besides, Lisette is not Jewish. She must've ordered her birth certificate from Grasse. Nazis recognize birth certificates as proof of race."

"Why is Mother staying in Paris?"

"There is your grandparents' apartment. Perhaps he is close to your mother and grandmother, and is afraid to send even a message to your mother. I know this is frightening news; however, your grandmother's a brave woman who will help determine the best course for all of you."

"We've been here longer than thirty days, Dona Grace, so why haven't we been forced to leave?"

"My old ties to powerful people remain strong. Many lives were helped by Pierre," says Dona Grace.

"He must have helped people in important government matters then, Dona Grace."

"Favors were primarily in the form of employment for relatives who were unable to find better-paying jobs. Moving from the fields to town was a goal of many young wives. In our first years here nearly seventy-per cent of the population lived outside of Lisbon and other larger cities. Even Antonio who made tiles for Pierre moved to Lisbon to take jobs, as Antonio did when he became our driver."

Just then Minna enters the drawing room and tries to speak a few Portuguese words.

"*Olá*, Dona Grace."

"*Olá*, Minna," responds Dona Grace as she welcomes Minna in her arms.

"*Olá*, Peter."

I play along, "*Olá*, Minna."

"*Como está*, Dona Grace?"

"I am very well, Minna! You are so bright! Who's teaching you Portuguese?"

"My friend, Kasia, is also from Warsaw. She knows Portuguese because her grandmother lives here." Minna bounces onto Dona Grace's lap. "Their whole family is here," sighs Minna.

"Your Bubbe just sent a telegram and she'll join you here soon."

"I want to kiss Bubbe's sweet cheek!" Then Minna stops and stutters, "But what about Mother and Father? We're all to be together."

"I think they will arrive a bit later, Minna," says Dona Grace. I try to believe that myself, but the direction of our escape seems to lack a final stop. *Where are we going to finally end the journey, so life will be normal again?*

Minna bites her lip to stop tears from springing out of her eyes.

"Minna, keep learning Portuguese, so you can surprise your parents," Dona Grace advises, to try to stop the tears in Minna's eyes.

Minna runs to the stairs before she begins to sob. I haven't thought of how alone she would feel at six years old, without her parents or grandparents.

Just then I remember the telegram stating, "Henri is at peace." For sure, Grandfather is no longer living, so we will not all be together ever again. *How can I now go back to painting our last Hanukkah celebration in Warsaw?*

Mezuzah, *Hebrew Word for Doorpost, Containing
a Small Scroll with Words from the Shema*

CHAPTER 11

Bubbe is Not the Same

Bubbe arrives by train one week later, but again, Antonio is sent to pick her up at the Estacao do Rossio station, instead of all of us meeting Grandmother. She might feel sad not to see us waiting with flowers or hugs, but Dona Grace understands that eyes are still watching, the *Estado Novo*, the New State, secret police. By December there are more uniformed police at the Lisbon train depots and a few officials are seen at markets.

Bubbe forgets to knock on Dona Grace's door, but she flies in and sweeps Minna into her arms. She doesn't lift Minna, but her skinny arms encircle all of Minna's body in a warm embrace. I move close to her, but stay back until Minna's sadness is swept back.

"Peter, you've really kept your family together these months alone!" exclaims Bubbe. She kisses me on both cheeks. "Minna still is the happy child."

"Ah, and you, my dearest friend from girlhood!" says Bubbe. She kisses Dona Grace on both cheeks. I never saw Bubbe kiss both cheeks like that until today.

"Oh, Peter, I see your confusion, but I am back to my French youth and ways. In France, this is the way of expressing affection, especially after such a long absence," says Bubbe, laughing gently at this unbelievable reuniting.

"*Olá*, Bubbe!" says Minna proudly.

"You're making great progress in your second new home since leaving Warsaw. I am amazed at how both of you have grown. You must be spending time on the beach. You have color in your face."

"Where is Grandfather?"

I haven't brought myself to deliver that sad news to Minna, so she doesn't know that only Mother remains in Paris, since Grandfather passed away weeks ago.

"Oh, I know, Mother would've been too alone without Grandfather." Minna answers her own question with a believable lie.

When will the truth be spoken to children?

Bubbe fingers the edge of her wool winter scarf and looks as though she might cry. I didn't like those scratchy wools when hugged as a little boy, but now I breathe in the damp woolen smell that is Bubbe in winter.

Rosanna enters the drawing room with a tray of hot chocolate for Minna and me with the blue flowered China cups of cappuccinos for Dona Grace and Bubbe.

We all sit together as Bubbe shares news from Paris with me. Dona Grace asks Minna to come to the patio to see the sun set.

"Is Mother safe with you gone, Bubbe?" I ask, concerned how my quiet mother would survive with her Jewish features.

"Peter, your mother looks like a German woman with her blond hair and smoked glasses. It may be difficult to explain the dark glasses as winter approaches. Now, her excuse is eye strain from reading music for so many years. I can't believe how easy it is to not tell the truth. Once a person begins to lie, it's easier and easier, and it's necessary in these strange times."

"Do the Paris police protect their people?"

"The Paris police actually work against the Jews and the Gypsies. Nazis ask French police to turn in their own people. Those who aid the Nazis are called 'collaborators.'"

"I can't understand how a policeman who knows his neighbors could help the Nazis."

"This is the problem with trust in Paris and probably everywhere the Nazis have infiltrated. Perhaps, Peter, we can talk about all of the details at another time." Bubbe's words become soft. Her intent is clearly to spare Minna any more shocks. Minna and Dona Grace return to our conversation in the drawing room.

"Does Mother remember me?" Minna asks Bubbe so quietly, Dona Grace doesn't seem to hear.

"I know she yearns to hold both of you. She feels if she waits just a bit longer, your father will contact her."

"How much longer, do you think?" My voice cracks when I speak and my breath becomes short.

"Life is changing too fast. It's like our lives are blurs. Later this week, Grace will take us all on a tour of Portugal. I'm eager to forget Paris and the troubles if even for a few hours," sighs Bubbe.

Bubbe seems to sleep almost every hour for two days, while we become more restless for our school break. It seems unreal that Hanukkah is skipped, but in Portugal, only Christmas is celebrated in 1939, with Nazi eyes everywhere.

Bubbe and Dona Grace plan for all of us to tour Portugal the last day before break. Dona Grace thinks it is exciting to take a day off when others aren't off. I'd never skipped school like this in Warsaw, but it is thrilling to break a rule.

This morning the yellow trolley will take us to the Sintra Hills; the weather is warm, sixty-degrees.

"Grace, I can't wait for today's tour: real castles on the hills, and fresh air from the Atlantic to breathe. It seems forever since I've been able to breathe. We never know who is watching us in Paris," says Bubbe.

Rede de eléctricos de Lisboa is the sign on the tram. We sit close together to hear Dona Grace, our tour guide, tell us about her favorite sites in Portugal.

"Look at *Praia da Adraga,* the elephant trunk cove." Dona Grace points quickly to the sea and outlines the shape of an elephant trunk so Minna can understand the cove's name.

If I were older, I, for sure, would investigate the many seaside caves in Portugal. My teacher, Mr. Kemlawski, talks about the thrill of cave expeditions, but cautions, "It's too cool in December for such exploration and the rains may cause flooding. Pirates left some of their *caches* in these caves. But don't go on your own. If you're here in the spring, we'll travel there for a school outing."

"I see a castle nearly hidden by trees," Minna spies the first castle.

"That's *Palacio National*, our oldest palace that is still standing. It is too bad that after 1910, the Monarchy fell and damage to the palace was immense," says Dona Grace.

"Look! There's another castle!" Bubbe is the first to notice the next castle.

"That's the *Castelo dos Mouros*, the Moors' Castle," says Dona Grace.

"Were Moors here first?" Geography is my next favorite school subject, but our class didn't discuss Moors thoroughly.

"The Moors ruled here until the 12th Century. The castle was built to hold back the Christian rulers during the *Reonquista*."

Minna gasps as the *Palacio da Pena* came into sight. "Oh! Oh!" is all she can say as she spies the colorful castle. Buildings in Warsaw are more practical, not so ornate.

"This is the *'piece de resistance,'*" says Dona Grace.

"Do you know what that means, Peter?" Bubbe asks.

"No." I try to guess: "The place to resist?"

Bubbe laughs her gentle laugh. "No, Peter, it is like the finest linen or the best dessert on the dessert tray."

"Look at the golden color, Peter!" says Dona Grace.

My eyes are nearly blinded by the design of *Palacio da Pena*. Gold paint covers most of the castle, but the windows below the black dome in the foreground are precise: three windows with white panes. The red trident-shaped tower contrasts with the half-circle dome.

"We'll get off here to walk the grounds," says Dona Grace.

Lush trees surround the Palace. "Are all of these trees native to Portugal?" I ask Dona Grace. There are such different sizes, shapes, and shades of greens.

"No, Peter. Trees here are ordered from many countries. There are sequoias from the United States, Chinese Ginko, fern trees from Australia and New Zealand," says Dona Grace.

One of the last sights is the Cruz Alta Cross, its tangled branches forming a sculpture at the end of the park.

Minna tugs on Bubbe's coat sleeve and asks, "Will we have lunch soon?"

I am also very hungry. Lunch is earlier at school, and even on weekends, lunch is served early. Rosanna sent a basket of sandwiches and oranges to enjoy on our return from the tour. I smile as I know she always includes sweet desserts for us.

CHAPTER 12

Our First Catholic Christmas

Although Hanukkah celebrations are forgotten, I can't forget Warsaw family preparations. If I close my eyes, I smell and taste Mother's mouth-watering warm *challah*.

Bubbe seems to revert to another time in her life. She's delighted to begin the Catholic preparations for Christmas. *Did she miss her Catholic Christmas Mass and early traditions when she married Grandfather?*

Rosanna calls the main dish, *"Consoada,"* the meal with codfish and vegetables including potatoes. Special pastries for our Christmas Eve dessert will be eaten after church, called *Missa do Galo* (Mass of the Rooster). When we return to Dona Grace's home, *Pay Natal,* or Father Christmas, will have left presents in the drawing room near the *Presépio,* the Nativity scene, and baby Jesus would be placed in the manger. In Dona Grace's home and in churches in Portugal the Nativity crèche doesn't include baby Jesus until Christmas Eve.

Bubbe claps her hands when we enter and she sees candles surrounding the *Presépio*.

Many gifts are wrapped with our names on tags. Never in Warsaw did we ever see this number of gifts. There are gifts for Antonio and Silvano, and Rosanna, and all of us. Bubbe bought Dona Grace perfume they remember from girlhood days.

I especially love the pastel sticks from Dona Grace. Soft colors will be an exciting inclusion. Charcoal is dramatic; however, the sea and the bull fight certainly require more emotion than my charcoal stick could capture.

Although Minna and I usually are asleep by nine o'clock, we, too, stay up for desserts. Dona Grace describes choices: the *Lampreia de ovos*, made with sugary egg yolks in the form of a fish, or *Filhos*, which is French toast. Also, Rosanna made the Bolo Res, the King Cake. There's a bean in the center of the cake and a small gift. If a person gets the bean, he or she is required to pay for the cake the next year. Minna laughs when her slice of cake shows the bean.

I wonder where will we be next year for the holidays. *Will our parents have joined us? How much longer will we be allowed in Lisbon with Dona Grace and Bubbe?* As I go to bed, I feel a chill.

I shouldn't have thought about next year during the second week of January 1940. We all feel there are more eyes on all of us, even in Dona Grace's home. Rosanna seems to linger near the table a bit more slowly after meals are served. Antonio seems to close the doors in the car more slowly. Bubbe and Dona Grace move chairs closer together as they drink afternoon tea on the weekends. I wonder what they talk about when we're gone.

Mr. Kemlawski conducts classes as usual; however, the due dates for long-term projects are not on the schedule. One of my classmates, Tymon, brings up the question in language class: "Mr. Kemlawski, will the research paper be due before or after Easter?"

"This project is detailed and will require much research, so I need to see when it will be possible for all of you to complete the work," Mr. Kemlawski answers in an uncharacteristic reply. He's organized and wants us to cover as much information and as many skills as possible since students come and go like a revolving door.

The impact of the war on schooling haunts him. Mr. Kemlawski mentions Adolph Hitler's belief that children only need to understand genetic purity and physical strength. I wish he would go into more detail, but those two goals are frightening enough. Genetic purity would mean only blond parents could have children. I'm not as physically strong as some students because students who live on farms are much stronger than I.

For two weeks we work on selecting an author we admire. Mr. Kemlawski reads short stories or chapters from novels to us. It's warm in the classroom and cool outside, so we should be able to concentrate on school, but Portugal's spring-like weather is just like Warsaw in spring when even I have a difficult time listening to a teacher read aloud.

Back in Warsaw the windows are pushed open enthusiastically. Teachers don't even ask me to open the window. We feel comfortable just adjusting for the cooler fragrant air to filter in. When my old Warsaw teacher, Mr. Bartels, reads his favorite poem of the day, even he seems to daydream with the beautiful words.

My choice of an author to research is still unclear. Romantic writers in Poland focus on social issues and revolutionary ideas. That type of literature really doesn't appeal to me since we're living those issues and their turmoil, and loneliness, and fear. This assigned long-term project does not excite me.

Now three weeks into 1940, our parents still have not arrived. Mother sends a letter this time that awaits when Minna and I arrive from school.

Once we're served our hot chocolate, we gather on a large overstuffed soft peach couch with Dona Grace. Bubbe sits in a wingback chair to read the letter to Minna and me.

> *Dear Mother, Dona Grace, Peter, and Minna,*
>
> *I'm missing all of you. My students are progressing on the violin beautifully."*

I know Mother is not exactly telling the truth. She's quite stingy with musical compliments. "Never listen to only the positive words, or you will never perfect your talents" is her comment on my art and Minna's violin lessons.

> *Many new neighbors. Every day the old neighbors leave, and new people move in immediately. Now when desirable locales open up, people move up. The new neighbors are from Charonne. It is strange to be without all of you.*
>
> *I await your return when the school year ends. One of the old power police came by to inquire when my children and Saul, my husband, will return.*

I recall Mother's sentence from the weird letter: "…Peter and Minna return after the school term in Lisbon ends, and Saul will return from Warsaw when the shop is secure."

Minna can't hold back tears from the rims of her eyes. Bubbe motions with her arms to come to her.

"Minna, Minna, life will all be better. It's been a long time since you were with your mother and father, but think how wonderful it will be when you are all together again." Bubbe does not look like she even believed it herself.

"Dona Grace, is it true that secret police here are enforcing the 30-day rule more closely with non-native Portuguese?" I ask, afraid to hear her response.

"There are such rumors, Peter, of the *Estado Novo,* Gestapo-like secret police."

"Grace, you still have great influence here, don't you?" asks Bubbe hurriedly.

"Yes, Lisette, those in power who are indebted to Pierre from long ago. Our relationships with old employees are strong, but new power, too, is strong, I fear," Dona Grace warns. "It is not easy to know who feels indebted to me because of Pierre, or if others may be influenced and swayed against me because of Nazi power."

"Why don't we all go down to the beach and enjoy today's sunshine?" suggests Bubbe as she gives Minna a strong hug. Then, she holds onto Minna's hands with her gnarled fingers. Arthritis bent her fingers, though they still long to play a violin.

As we walk, we see a dark-haired girl with a stringed instrument on the corner playing a haunting tune. A colorful red and gold box holds a few *escudos*. Across the street an older boy watches us carefully. I wonder if he, like me, is the protector of his sister.

"Isn't her instrument beautiful, Minna?" asks Dona Grace, trying to distract Minna from her lingering tears.

"That doesn't look like anything I've seen," says Minna. "It isn't the same shape as my violin."

"The pear shape and ornate scroll are features of the Coimbra guitar," says Dona Grace.

"Do you remember when I told you about our *Fado* music, Minna?"

"I remember," mumbles Minna as her eyes lock on the girl's fingers on the strings.

Strong music transforms Minna back to Mother's lessons in Warsaw. She really craves her music.

Our walk put all of us in a better mental place by the time we open Dona Grace's front door. Transformed by the softer winter light and the darker color of the Atlantic Ocean, the subtle light lifts my heart.

CHAPTER 13

Bubble and Dona Grace Have a Plan

Mr. Kemlawski is gone on Monday morning. A young female teacher stands next to his desk and tells us that she is our new teacher.

"Where is he?" I ask.

She shakes her head and says, "I am not allowed to discuss teacher or student information." She presses her upper and lower lips into a shocking red line, coated with heavy lipstick, to let me know there will not be any discussion about Mr. Kemlawski.

Dominik comes up to me at recess. "Come over to the fence of the school yard, ok? I heard that Mr. Kemlawski's family arranged for a passport for him to the United States."

"Why'd Mr. Kemlawski leave Portugal? He wants to return to Warsaw once the war ends," I ask.

"There are rumors about Jews being transported to camps from the ghettos," replies Dominik. He turns slightly, so Tymon can't hear us.

"Why are Jews rounded up?" I ask.

"There are ugly rumors about that. Even children. Men and women sent separately. No one cares if children are separated from parents," Dominik says. "My parents are trying to get passports to Central America this week."

I wonder if Bubbe and Dona Grace are discussing sending Minna and me away.

When Minna and I arrive home, Dona Grace takes Minna's hand as they walk to the patio for hot chocolate. Bubbe leads me into the drawing room. Today, I notice the ornate frames on the original paintings of the sea in this room.

For some reason, my eyes always focus only on the image inside the frame, but boundaries must be on my mind.

"Peter, Grace and I are contacting people to move you and Minna as quickly as possible out of Portugal."

The swell of the ocean in the painting imitates the feeling in my stomach. It feels like a lurch starts at the pit of my stomach and is surging upwards.

I shift in my chair and stare at my feet on the floor. Then I tell her, "When I went into my classroom this morning, our teacher, Mr. Kemlawski, was gone. A new teacher came into the room."

"Is a reason given for his departure?"

"She says she is not allowed to speak about other teachers."

"Are other students missing from class today?" Bubbe asks.

"No, but one of my classmates said his parents are obtaining visas and transport to go to Central America very soon."

"These discussions are everywhere in Lisbon."

"Won't you travel with us?" I ask with a gasp at this new life alone with Minna. *Could this be my dream/nightmare of that far-off place with no adults? Frightening!*

"I need to ensure that Chana and Saul are also safe," says Bubbe slowly and hesitatingly. *Bubbe's thinking like a mother for her daughter's safety. Apparently, grandchildren are on their own.*

"We'll all join together, Peter. I promise on your grandfather's memory."

"Where are we being sent?"

"For your safety, we can't tell you yet. It will be safe. You'll be with a Jewish family in a neutral country."

"Aren't we going to one of the Americas?"

"That I can tell you is not the case. We're sending you to a closer country. Again, for your safety and your parents' safety, the destination must be secret. If you and your parents are too far apart, especially in different countries, it might take years for you to find each other."

Minna burst in the room to tell me that Dona Grace was taking all of us for a special dinner.

"Peter, *Tavares Rico* restaurant is the oldest in Lisbon. It opened in 1817."

Our move has to be coming even sooner than I thought.

Next morning at school two classmates are missing. No teacher comes into the room as the bell rings, so we cluster in groups, or pairs, just talking.

I ask Dominik behind my cupped hand, "Where'd Mr. Kemlawski go?"

He moves closer and whispers, "My father heard he was smuggled from Lisbon to Dublin, Ireland."

"Didn't he have a passport to meet with his family in the United States?"

"How'd you know his parents and the rest of the family escaped to America?" Dominik's raised left eyebrow reveals shock that I knew the Kemlawski family's destination.

"Mr. Kemlawski told the whole class."

"I mustn't have been here in Lisbon then," said Dominik.

A new boy in a uniform of a short sleeved green shirt and tan shorts stands out from the rest of us who wear long pants and sweaters over our shirts. He wears a medal pinned to a green and red striped ribbon.

I look carefully but can't see the letters on the medal as he enters our classroom. He hasn't been in class before today. Instead of keeping his eyes on the floor as most new students do, he looks carefully at each student for just one minute too long.

"Watch out for him," Tymon says. "He's in the *Mocidade Portuguese.*"

"What's that?"

"It's a youth movement here in Portugal. They give lists of refugees who overstay the thirty-day rule to the Lisbon police," says Tymon.

"What does this group do?"

"I don't understand, Peter, but it's growing quickly. There are different age levels: the youngest are called *Lusitos* who are seven to ten years of age. That boy is our age so they are called *Infants* until they are fourteen."

How does Dona Grace have special permission for Minna and me to stay so long?

Dominik's eyes blink over and over to indicate this boy was close to us.

He walks up to me and asks, "Where are you from?"

Mr. Kemlawski's replacement stands directly in front of us, tapping a pointer on the desk, so we stop talking.

My mind won't stay on the math problem the young teacher wrote on the board. *Why would Jews move from Lisbon to Dublin?*

I needn't wonder long as Bubbe and Dona Grace both look directly at me when Minna and I return from school.

Bubbe says, "Minna, come with me into the kitchen for a treat."

"What's the treat, Bubbe?"

"You'll need to wait to see."

Dona Grace motions for me to sit next to her on the settee. "Peter, your grandmother and I are making arrangements to move you and Minna for your safety."

With a gulp, I ask, "When?"

"As soon as possible. The *Estado Novo* are watching carefully now for extended leaves of Jewish visitors."

I hate the idea of racing again to escape the Nazis. Every move is farther from our home in Warsaw. The possibility of my family returning to home seems impossible for our lifetime.

"Does that mean the secret police?"

"Yes, Peter. There are spies everywhere and Minna's features are noticeable as is her musical ability. We can't hide her. Your fair hair and blue eyes must be from your grandmother's family. The rest of the family were French, but Lisette's grandmother was English."

"Where is it safe?" I pause before I tell Dona Grace about my teacher's escape. "My friend, Dominik, says our teacher took a boat from here to Dublin. And today a new boy in a uniform joined our class. Dominik told me to watch out for him. We couldn't talk any more about Mr. Kemlawski."

"How amazing your friend knew that! Lisette sent for her French birth certificate this week. In France there are lists being compiled of non-French Jews. Who knows how safe anyone with Jewish blood will be?"

"Will Grandmother travel with us?"

"It's impossible. She needs her birth certificate. Lisette is waiting until your mother and father join us here in Lisbon.

Dona Grace has the knowledge and wisdom to understand Lisbon. I hate the idea of racing again to escape the Nazis. Every move takes us further from my home. I feel burning in my stomach that will not go away for some time.

Havdalah, *a ceremony marking the end of Shabbat, includes lighting a special Havdalah candle with several wicks and having a cup of wine*

CHAPTER 14

Minna Shows the Fear I Can't Shake

For the next two days, Minna and I go to school, but Minna doesn't chatter as usual. Dona Grace says little in the morning and Bubbe stares out the window, so I only nod as Minna waits for my responses to her brief questions.

Bubbe's usual, "We'll see you after school," is replaced by "Goodbye for now."

Dona Grace turns her back while Bubbe stares at the floor as we leave.

The day is long. Dominik is absent today. *Did he leave as abruptly as Mr. Kemlawski?* It's as though I never knew them. It is like looking at an image in a mirror that fades away: They have disappeared from my life.

A man sitting in the drawing room with Bubbe and Dona Grace is dressed shabbily in clothes smelling of the sea. Dark olive green moss clings to the edge of his trousers, and he smells of brine. *What's happening?*

Dona Grace says, "You'll have to trust Danilo, Peter."

I can't speak. Minna just stares. She has not been so terrified since leaving Warsaw. Her eyes speak of loss both real and imagined. I think imagined fear and loss are more real than reality, as I try to turn off my mind's racing images and sounds.

Our time with Dona Grace in Portugal is like a refuge in the midst of war. We didn't think about bombings, or roundups, or shootings. *What's awaiting us? Is there news about Mother and Father? Probably not, if there is a man waiting for our return from school.*

Bubbe looks as though her heart is held in place by barbed wire. She knows unfortunately what Nazis plan for those they round up. Those articles from newspapers hint at as much. She contains her terror only with that faint awkward smile, for Minna's sake.

"Danilo's father worked for my husband for many years. He is our most trusted friend for the longest time. Danilo works on coasters, smaller boats, taking goods to Dublin. The Lisbon Run has been in place for a few months. He is taking you and Minna to a Jewish settlement."

"When will we leave?" I ask in a choked voice.

"You'll leave as soon as the sun sets, Peter," says Dona Grace, in such a firm tone that I'm startled.

"Are Mother and Father in trouble?" I'm afraid to hear the answer as I clasp my hands tightly behind my back.

"We don't know," answers Bubbe slowly, rubbing the knuckles on her left hand.

"Minna and I have never traveled on the sea." I worry for both of us.

"Since both Ireland and Lisbon are neutral, we want you to leave quickly."

"Have we been reported for staying too long, Dona Grace?" I ask.

"Antonio has heard rumors about the *Estado Novo* asking about you and Minna's extended stay," replies Dona Grace.

I look at Bubbe. "How will we ever see Mother and Father again?"

"We have a plan that is so fragile, Peter, that we are afraid to say it aloud," says Dona Grace.

I realize this is no time to be a hero. I'm a child, less likely to take charge. Children don't have any power unless they cry or scream, but I am too old for that.

Our parents are gone. Grandfather is buried without us saying goodbye, and Bubbe is so changed since she became a young girl again in Dona Grace's home. Now, she is always reliving her days at the perfume counter.

A braver son might try to sneak back to France to at least see Mother. Like Father, I calculate risk. I even believe like Father that if you always follow law and don't stand out, you will be left alone. It doesn't appear Father and I are right about being quiet and left alone.

Throughout this discussion, Danilo sits quietly, studying the cap he twirls too quickly in his hands. I guess he's worried that the sun is nearly down and we don't have our bags, and we haven't come close to saying our goodbyes.

"Good friends of Danilo will invite you to join their son and daughter until you can join your parents. Ireland does not call this time a World War: In Ireland, it's 'The Emergency,'" says Dona Grace.

"It certainly is an emergency, but no bombs fall," are the first words spoken by Danilo.

"We're free to travel, Peter and Minna." Danilo's the first person to talk to Minna directly. This is very kind of him.

"Our freight runs have been peaceful, so far no challenges by the Germans."

"Germans need tungsten from Portugal for their war efforts," says Dona Grace. "There is a dance now between

Germany and Britain for Portugal's most valuable natural resource."

Danilo stands up to signal that it's time to leave. I'm so hungry normally after school, but I'm too numb to know if the feeling in my stomach is hunger or fear. I notice Rosanna is not here and neither is Antonio. *Are they included in the number of possible spies?*

Are collaborators in France trying to seek out any escaped Jews? Is money such a motivator that loyalty and friendship are forgotten? What is the price of turning in Jewish refugees who overstay their thirty days? What about Antonio's sharing the bull fight with me? What about Rosanna's delicious hot chocolate? Doesn't Rosanna understand what will happen to Minna if we are sent back to Warsaw? Everyone now knows about the Warsaw ghetto for Jews, and many Jews in Poland have been sent away on trains.

Bubbe hands me Minna's old brown suitcase and another plain dark blue suitcase with food and supplies.

"You're the strong one, Peter. Check the blue suitcase for insurance for you and Minna," says Bubbe, hinting there are jewels inside of the case.

"Take care, dear Minna," says Dona Grace.

"My dear, my dear, Minna," stutters Bubbe.

Neither Minna nor I speak. We're both in shock.

Danilo speaks French, Portuguese, and English from his contacts with his many food markets. He tries to calm our fears as we walk toward the Lisbon Marina with his frequent smiles. The small boat's a surprise to me.

"Is this the boat we'll be on?" I ask Danilo.

"It's called a coaster, Peter. It's designed for the Lisbon Run. We won't be out of sight of land, so if the weather is especially harsh, we'll make for land. It's being loaded with fruits, wheat for cattle from South and North America, Portugal, and Spain," said Danilo. We see silhouettes of strong men hoisting crates of goods at the marina.

I know why we left Dona Grace's home in the dark: There are few eyes except those hoisting goods.

"Hey, Danilo, what's with the kids?" asks a man lifting an extremely heavy load.

"They're my niece and my nephew from Dublin. Going back home again after visiting their grandmother."

The man takes this in stride and doesn't stare at us. After seeing the new boy at school in the *Mocidade Portuguese*, I'm too watchful.

Danilo guides us up the plank onto the deck. Men near the sides of the coaster pull crates of fruit up from the adjacent ship from South America. It's so dark even outlines of mariners can't be seen.

"Careful as we walk to the aft of the boat not to bump into ropes," says Danilo. "Most of the goods are already packed in the hold," he explains, pointing to the center of the coaster. Both Minna and I are tired, and yet hungrier by now as we see the satchel Rosanna sent for our picnic to the Sintra Hills.

"Peter, you and your sister need to eat the sandwiches and drink the juice before you sleep," says Danilo as he unpacks the bag from Dona Grace. He gives the waxed paper wrapped sliced beef sandwich to Minna.

"I just want to lie down and close my eyes," she says.

"Danilo's right, Minna, we need to eat first. The boat will rock quite often, won't it, Danilo?"

He hands me the sandwich for dinner and asks, "Haven't you both been on a boat before?"

"No, neither of us. I don't think my mother has been on a boat either," says Peter.

"Minna, you must eat now in case you have difficulty keeping food in your stomach," answers Danilo with a worried look.

How rocky will this trip be?

"This boat will duck into land if the weather is especially rough. Not to worry. Do you like to swing?" Danilo asks Minna.

"Yes, I love to swing with my friend Kasia."

"The boat will feel like swinging. Try to think of being with your friend on a swing," says Danilo.

"Now, I won't see that friend ever again, will I, Peter?" asks Minna as tears brim her lower eye lids.

"Minna, I honestly don't know where we will end up, but I believe we'll be with Mother and Father again sometime."

The deck of the boat feels smooth, but I hear puddles as we walk on the deck in the dark. Danilo has blankets for us but spreads a canvas underneath us, so we won't be damp and cold.

I stay awake until I hear Minna's regular soft breaths, and then I go out like a light had been switched off. No dreams for me that night. Minna moves closer to my blanket and I put my arm around her shoulders. Then I, too, am in a hard sleep.

Before full dawn, the boat lurches. I squint my eyes until the light and my eyes adjust. I can see this marina's huge as we leave Lisbon.

"You're awake, Peter," says Danilo. "I want you to see *'The Exposicao do Mundo Portugues.'* It's being completed for the June Exposition. Sculptures carved of wood and plaster show our Portuguese discoverers: Vasco da Gama who found the route to India, Ferdinand Magellan who sailed around the world, and many other Portuguese heroes."

Minna's terrified scream pierces the air. "Where are we, Peter?" She's still on the deck in the blankets, but she doesn't know why we're moving. The morning light is too bright for Minna, so she covers her eyes with her hands.

"It'll be all right, Minna," I say as I hurry forward to stop her terror, and to keep those on board from looking at us.

"I only remember leaving Bubbe and Dona Grace," Minna shakes her head to try to remember the walk and the dark and the sandwich."

The boat moves quietly and smoothly alongside the enormous monument.

Those figures are detailed and so smooth, I yearn to touch them.

Minna's shocked eyes reveal too many changes for such a young child. She hasn't chattered since our walk to school yesterday.

Nazis came too fast. The first of September, troops started to march, and eight days later we began running for what will last for a long time. Names from geography class have become my homes: France, Portugal, and now, Dublin.

CHAPTER 15

Minna Is Terrified

"Will we really be OK, Danilo?" I ask him. Minna creeps across the deck away from the boxes. She sits calmly, actually, too calmly. She looks like a frozen statue.

"You're going to a section of Dublin where Jewish people have lived for many years."

"Will Minna be safe there?" I ask, remembering Father asking, or was it commanding, me to protect Minna.

"You'll live with the Leib family. I'll return frequently to bring letters from Dona Grace and your grandmother. You may send letters back to them. This is the safest place for you and Minna for now. When your parents join your grandmother in Portugal, the plan for your family's escape will be put in motion."

I feel oddly comforted even though there is no date for my family's reunion.

Danilo turns back toward the captain as heavy grey clouds billow on the horizon.

A strong wind comes up so quickly that Minna is thrown across the deck. I run to hold her in place and rub the patterned quilt around her arms. We wear winter coats, but wind in Poland isn't icy like these small needle-like gusts.

Danilo walks back to us after speaking with the captain. "Our captain also knew Dona Grace and her husband well. He'll ensure you're safe on the Atlantic Ocean. Take a rest on the deck," says Danilo. "The wind won't bite your cheeks when you are lower on the deck."

"Peter, I'm so afraid." Minna's eyes don't have that wide-eyed fear as yesterday, but her eyes are red from the wind and dried tears. "Do you think we'll ever see Warsaw again and be a family again?"

"In my heart, I can't see Warsaw for us, Minna, but I think after a time Mother and Father will meet up with us. We may be alone for some time, but I'll always take care of you. Do you remember when Father left Paris? He told me to 'watch out' for you always."

"I remember, Peter, but you aren't old enough, are you?"

All those geography lessons of far-off lands have come true. Honestly, I never thought I would leave Poland. Since

Grandfather and Bubbe left Warsaw for Paris, I thought we might go there for vacations once the threat of the Nazis passed, but I planned for us to return home to Warsaw.

That's how Father described the end of the conflict with Adolph Hitler. Jews didn't think Hitler could overtake Poland. Certainly, not France nor Spain, nor who knew where this will end.

Minna stares waiting for me to answer her question.

"Yes, I am, Minna. When you are the oldest in the family, you always are responsible for the little one."

My emotions hide. This is good and this is a terrible weight. It is good to feel strongly, but I need to always think of Minna's tender heart. Always I am the protector.

Danilo follows my eyes focusing on the castle in the distance. "That is Malahide Castle, Peter. Ireland has more than 30,000 remains of castles and many grand ones still stand. You may visit them while you live here."

"Live here? I thought we're just stopping for a short time, Danilo."

"If you are here for even a short time, think of yourselves as living here, Peter. You'll enjoy much more freedom than Paris and even Lisbon hold for Jewish people."

As we enter Dublin's frantic port there's so much talking, singing, and laughing in a language I haven't heard before. I glance up and see a looming castle. The mist-like rain is falling. We're in the place I dreamed of so long ago: strange language, and a castle, and Minna and I are alone.

Shock! Seeing the castle. Feeling the mist. This is my dream come to life. It still frightens me as the dreams did back as a child in Warsaw. So vivid. Now, so real.

The worst part of this is that I know Mother and Father won't be here with Minna and me. I know I'll never be a child again. I'm responsible for myself, but more seriously, even, I'm now responsible for my six-year-old sister.

With the haunting image of the Gypsies' mid-morning escape in Warsaw, I sense life's going to change for the worst for everyone. *How can one group of people be rounded up like animals, and the rest of humanity think they'll not be vulnerable?*

I want to say, "No. I can't even take care of myself in another new country. These people are Catholics, serious Catholics. St. Patrick, a Roman, converted them. Will other people try to convert us to Catholicism?"

I haven't had friends since living in Warsaw. Mother and Father really never seemed to have close friends. I never considered that before. *Did they have friends like Dona Grace and*

Bubbe were way back when they were young? Could Richard and I be friends again when we are old?

My face must have shown all these questions because Danilo asked me twice, "Are you ok?"

Being fourteen, I have never before been on any boat, never anywhere without both of our parents. Minna's eyes fix on a castle and she almost smiles. She's thinking of a princess story.

I shiver from the cold wind and rain and the realization that my haunting dream has come to be reality. As I look down at this waterway, Danilo speaks in awe. "This is the River Liffey, Peter."

The huge river's full of boats coming and going, and there are a few people fishing from the bank. The men look so relaxed standing on the banks holding their poles.

"Brown trout are plentiful here beginning in March," Danilo says. "Have you fished before?"

"Yes, when my grandmother, Bubbe, and my grandfather still lived in Warsaw we fished along the River Wisla near our home. Sometimes during Rosh Hashanah rabbis prayed along the shore."

"I would imagine you were a good fisherman, since you are alert and patient."

"Dona Grace's kind, Danilo, but it feels temporary there. I want to be in a place where my family is together and where there aren't eyes waiting to check out Minna's dark hair and dark eyes."

"You know, Peter, there are Travelers here who are dark-haired, and some Irish have black hair. Some of the dark-haired even have blue eyes. These black-haired people are called the Black Irish. Minna won't stand out as she did in Paris."

"Right. Minna just blended in with her hair color and dark eyes in Lisbon."

"As soon as the goods in this boat are unloaded, we'll meet with your new hosts."

While Danilo works with crates up and down the plank, Minna and I walk slowly for a short distance along the River Liffey. The long bridge brings one side of Dublin to the next. The bridge's scroll work is intricate, and the bridge blends into the gray sky. The air's fresh, but I fear eyes peeking through the clouds.

There are padlocks with initials hooked to the bridge. *What're these for?* Locks of any type seem frightening now.

When the last crate's unloaded, Danilo comes down the bridge to us.

"This is the Ha'penny Bridge, Minna. Do you know what a ha'penny is?" asks Danilo as he bends down to look into Minna's eyes.

Minna shakes her head back and forth.

"We don't have such a thing," answers Peter.

"It's a coin paid for crossing the bridge. Before the Bridge was built in 1892, people had to wait for a ferry, or take a long route." Danilo turns his head to me to explain the charge for crossing. "There was a charge to the builder, Walsh, in case the bridge failed. The ha'penny was to pay for another new bridge. No charge now."

"What're the locks there?" I point to the rows of locks on the Bridge.

"Those are love locks with the keys thrown away to show lovers plan to be together for all time, Peter," says Danilo with a laugh. "See the initials. Some lovers carve their initials on tree trunks in other towns, but here they have love locks."

"Danilo," I move closer to him to ask him about money for Minna and me now that Bubbe and Dona Grace are in Portugal, and we're in another country. "Did Bubbe tell you how Minna and I are to pay for our keep here?" I am uncomfortable speaking about this after such a long journey that could've caused trouble for Danilo and his ship's captain.

"I thought Dona Grace and your grandmother would have spoken to you about the arrangement. Sorry, you've been worried, Peter. There is a letter for the Leib family and a letter to you. You and your host family are to read it together. Dona Grace said to tell you after we landed in Dublin that you will be provided for very well. You're not to worry about money for yourself and Minna."

After a walk that was slow with Minna's smaller steps on red brick roads, we arrive on North Strand Street. I thought I smelled sweet *challah* bread. *Did I imagine this?*

Crowds mingle in the streets. We hear quiet sing-song lilted voices, then Jewish voices talking and then fuller Jewish laughs. Our family didn't have such laughs. Our laughter was based more on subtle humor, I guess.

"Here's the Leib house." Danilo raises the knocker as Minna hides behind me.

"Good morning," says a woman, opening the door and welcoming us. She wears a yellow floral buttoned-up house dress and black laced shoes with a short heel.

"Good morning, Mrs. Leib," says Danilo.

"Welcome, children!" Mrs. Leib replies in Yiddish.

"Mrs. Leib, this is Minna." Danilo gestures with his open hand. "And this is Peter Knobel."

"So kind of you, Mrs. Leib," I say looking directly into her eyes. The familiar language alone makes me feel welcome, and her apron with sprinkles of flour reminds me of Mother.

"You must feel uncertain now, Peter and Minna, but our family will love having you here with us."

I'm tired of worrying about Minna and myself and my parents.

Then I catch my breath: I must make the very best of this time. It doesn't feel as temporary as Lisbon did. This must be a happy time with this family in this beautiful city. No bombs dropping. It doesn't seem like there are eyes anywhere.

We are not in Warsaw or even Paris with Nazis at the heels of running Jews. There is fresh food—not served by Rosanna like in Lisbon, but there is a family who doesn't have to lock their doors. I need wisdom to make the very best of the situation. I will try not to worry about Mother and Father. Yet, I want to be young.

Danilo waves at us and turns, "I'll return in one week from today, Peter and Minna. Your grandmother and Dona Grace will send messages."

"Please remind them to send my violin with you!" says Minna in a strained whisper. She must be missing her music.

CHAPTER 16

My Old Teacher Is Now My New Teacher

"Ah, Minna, we love music," Mrs. Leib says. "Come in. You're in the land of music. The Irish love to sing, pick, and dance to violins."

For the first time in a very long week, Minna's lips look like she might smile, but her eyes look like she is close to tears. I can't imagine being six, nearly seven now—I recall her birthday is soon. My fourteenth birthday has come and gone during these hectic months.

"Come in the kitchen, children." I hadn't thought of myself as a child even in Warsaw because Jewish boys at thirteen are responsible to follow commandments. Even by my twelfth birthday, I felt responsible, and by April 1940, I am an adult with my nearly six-year-old sister's life in my hands. *Child?* I can't believe I ever thought of myself as a child.

"I baked *challah* for this special day for you, our guests." Mrs. Leib intones a *hamotzi*, a blessing, over the *challah*.

With the first bite, Mother's peach jam and our family's race into the forest flash before me. This bread tastes delicious, but slightly different than Mother's *challah*. We have not eaten *challah* for many months.

"My husband is running our grocery store," says Mrs. Leib. "Our children are close to your ages. Steph is sixteen and Ruth is eight. They will love having you here."

"Will we attend school, Mrs. Leib?" I ask.

"Of course, Peter. Both of you will attend school. Our Rabbi found a teacher from Poland."

"Where in Poland?"

"I believe he first taught in Warsaw." Mrs. Leib thinks for a moment and then the realization on her face that we lived in Warsaw causes her to smile. "Maybe you will be acquainted with this teacher."

With silent prayer, I hope it will be Mr. Bartels.

"His name is Mr. Bartels," says Mrs. Leib.

"He's my favorite teacher, Mrs. Leib." My right knee trembles as I think of all the changes in the course of six months. How amazing it is that my teacher would come back into my life. School is so hit and miss, but here in Ireland—my old teacher from Warsaw. *How strange is that? Coincidence?*

"He is the instructor in the synagogue school. Six synagogues for us here in Dublin, and your school is close to our home."

"Our Jewish community even has a Jewish tailors' union, and the Bretzel Bakery has been in business since the 1800s. There are more Catholics than Jews here, but this is not Germany, thankfully, Peter."

I saw Mrs. Leib glance over as Minna sits quietly pulling at the end of the slice of *challah*. Even the delicious sweetness can't erase her confusion with this latest move.

"Don't you like my bread, Minna?" asks Mrs. Leib.

"Thank you, but I'm not very hungry," says Minna.

"Minna is confused since we came by boat, Mrs. Leib. We had never been on a train or a boat in our lives until these last few months. Many places and new people, but we are grateful to you and your family."

"Minna, are you excited to have a good friend now? Ruth will be like a sister."

"Does Ruth play music, Mrs. Leib?" asks Minna with more enthusiasm than she had showed before.

"Ruth plays a bodhran. That is an Irish drum," replies Mrs. Leib. "Our Ruth is a lively lass for sure."

"I've never heard of that instrument," Minna shrugs her shoulders and stares at me to see if I have heard of a bodhran.

"No, Minna, I do not know that instrument." I shake my head. "How's it played, Mrs. Leib?"

"It's a circular drum made of goat skin. The skin is tacked on one side; the other side is left open to control the pitch. Some have a bone to use, but Ruth keeps time with her knuckles."

"Let me show you the bedrooms. Peter, you'll share the room with Stephan, and Minna, you and Ruth will share a room," says Mrs. Leib. She opens the first bedroom for Minna.

"If you like, Minna, why don't you rest before Ruth comes flying in to meet you?"

Minna still looks wide-eyed, but her shoulders relax now. Her shoulders were nearly up to her ears since the boat from Portugal first cast off.

"Peter, we'll try to show Minna extra care since she is so young. Don't you worry yourself."

"Thank you, Mrs. Leib, I'll rest in Stephan's room until he comes home if that's OK."

"Please feel free while you are in our home. There is always room in our home for anyone needing a warm place and a warm meal."

After winter months of corned beef and cabbage, and Irish stew, becoming accustomed to our new home, we sit in the living room listening to the BBC radio report. The door knocker startles me; however, Stephan and Ruth ignore the sound, until Mr. Leib says, "Stephan, could you get the door, please?"

Danilo stands in the doorway with a large envelope. His promise to bring us a letter after two weeks back in January was not kept. I never told Stephan or Mrs. Leib that I was waiting for many weeks to learn about our parents and grandmother, and Dona Grace. Each week I add another mental diagonal line to my count. For such a large gap in letters, something must be wrong somewhere.

"So good to see that Peter and Minna fit right in," says Danilo.

"You know, Danilo, Mr. Leib and I always hoped for even more children. Peter and Minna are like the brother to Stephan and the sister to Ruth they did not have before."

"Well, this is a long letter judging from the weight of it," Danilo says, handing the letter to Mrs. Leib who then passes the packet to Peter. "I'll return tomorrow evening to pick up a letter if you wish to respond to your grandmother and Dona Grace. Good night."

"It's your family, Peter, and you are the proper person to read the letter. Do you want to go to your bedroom to read it alone before sharing it with Minna?"

"Mrs. Leib, I'd feel more comfortable if you read it to us."

Mrs. Leib says, "Thank you, Peter, for your trust." She reaches for a letter opener on the dark desk near the window. She clears her throat and begins.

Dearest Peter and Minna,

The weather here is lovely. Soft breezes and gentle rains. No news from the forest, but many new thirty-day residents arrive daily. Those who stay beyond the thirty-day limit are sent back to their native lands. Grace and I wait for my birth certificate but have not yet received it. The musician is still with students in Paris. The musician says the apartment is large and empty without you and Minna. No more cornichons on sandwiches or pastel macaroons for those on Montmartre. Nazis purchase the most delectable treats and also essentials, so those of us in queues wait to reach the counter, where very little is left for us to buy.

There are clippings from the newspaper of the war accounts showing more details than I wish to write. Please decide which stories are of interest to you, but avoid those that might frighten Minna. We await your letter to us.

Love, Bubbe and Dona Grace

Minna jumps up from the floor with a whimper and a gasp. Ruth follows her out of the living room, but Ruth returns quickly because Minna holds the bedroom door shut with her shoulder.

"I think Minna needs some quiet time before your *craic*," Mrs. Leib tells Ruth.

"I see you haven't yet heard the Irish word for fun, yet, Peter," says Mrs. Leib, noticing the question in my eyes.

Fun? I think fun is only for young children who don't know better.

"Do you know what your grandmother meant?" asks Mr. Leib.

"Our Mother has not left Paris. Our father must still be hiding, so Bubbe tells us the woods or a hiding place do not allow Father to contact Mother. Food must not be as delicious as when we visited our grandparents in Paris. My grandfather took me for a pastry on Montmartre. Our grandmother, Bubbe, and Dona Grace must still hide details, so instead of writing about the war, there are clippings from various newspapers."

I picture Mother sitting at the corner of the curtain peeking through a slit to watch the Gestapo. *Does she think she will catch the first glimpse of Father? Will she recognize him without his beard, or does he still shave to try to eliminate his Jewish beard? Will she enjoy a family dinner like Mrs. Leib prepares every night? Does Bubbe worry about Mother as I worry about Mother and Father every single night before sleep comes, so slowly?*

"Can you read French, Peter?" Mr. Leib asks.

"A little," I say as I examine the photos in the clippings.

"Tell me later about the news," says Mr. Leib.

Danilo returns the following night at the exact time he came the night before.

"Are you allowed to transport foods as easily as before?" Mr. Leib asks Danilo.

"We've not been stopped, but there are reports that some Irish vessels are stopped and examined. Hopefully, I'll return in a month to bring a new message.

Challah, *Jewish Braided Bread, Often Eaten at Ceremonies*

CHAPTER 17

Stephan, the Brother I Always Wanted

Stephan is taller than I, and he is a jokester. I wonder if the good humor of the Irish people rubbed off on this Jewish family. Our family is generally serious.

After dinner, Stephan asks me, "How do you like living in the Pale?"

"Does that have to do with the dim sunlight, Stephan?" I ask.

"No, that is the nickname for Dublin," Stephan answers. "Please call me Steph. All my friends do. I'll think my parents are chiding my cheekiness if you call me Stephan."

"Right!"

"I'll ask Da about our whole family spending next Sunday at Phoenix Park," Steph says.

"Is the name from Greek mythology?" I ask.

"No, the Irish, the Gaelic language somehow was misused. 'Phoenix' is said to refer to the warm underground springs found on the grounds. Would you and Minna like to see our zoo?"

"There are many huge but also many small animals," Ruth chimes in as she hears our conversation.

"What animal is your favorite, Ruth?" asks Minna.

"I love the tapirs!"

"We didn't have tapirs in our Warsaw Zoo," answers Minna, though nobody listens to her because everyone is thinking of their favorite animal.

"I think the elephants are the best of all the animals," says Steph, ignoring Minna.

"Do you go to the zoo often?" I ask.

"We usually go during the summer, but with mild weather this month due to warm winds from Spain, Father wants to go early this year."

"Is the park way far away?" asks Minna, remembering the beautiful but rather long day for her in Lisbon's Sintra Hills Park.

"Phoenix Park is barely outside of Dublin. It's huge and before the war there were international race car events there," says Steph.

"Dinner is ready," calls Mrs. Leib. She sets down a large bowl of vegetables and beef.

"Smells delicious!" Steph says. The gravy was hearty, like food in Warsaw.

"Irish stew!" says Mr. Leib as Steph hands his plate to his father for a serving. Dishes are all passed to him, and then back to each of us before we say a blessing for the meal.

It feels quite comfortable in this house with a regular Jewish family. Not like our family or like our much larger house in Warsaw, but the gathering's pleasant and ordinary. All of our meals with Dona Grace were carefully prepared, but meals there are not as fun as tonight's dinner in Dublin.

Steph and I wash the dinner dishes, and Ruth and Minna dry the dishes, forks, and spoons, then everything is put away. All four of us go outside for the last of the warm evening. Mr. and Mrs. Leib move into the living room to relax and talk with each other.

A group of children in the lane are playing marbles on the cobblestones. *How can the marbles be controlled on cobblestones?*

"Come over here." Steph motions me to hunch down next to him. "Here's a blue cat eye for you."

"Could I hold one up to see the beautiful colored curve inside the marble?" Minna asks.

"Sure, here's a yellow one for you."

"Don't I get one, too?" demands Ruth with a huff.

"Where's your bag with marbles, Ruth?" Steph asks.

"I lost all of mine last week at school recess."

"Here's a few for you and Minna until you win some yourselves," says Steph.

"Minna hasn't played marbles because she's only six and wasn't at school."

"Minna, the idea is to tick someone else's marble with your marble, and then you get to keep the marble your marble hits. You say 'keepsies.'"

"Does everyone here have marbles?" I ask.

"Oh, sure, my father sells these at our store. He'll give you and Minna a sack of marbles."

"Ah, that is so beautiful: that curve of yellow in the tiny ball," says Minna.

"That is called a banana marble," answers Ruth.

"Now, watch, Minna." James, the next-door neighbor boy, flicks his thumb on the top of his index finger to shoot the marble toward another boy's marble.

James's marble bounces on the cobblestones. The other boy aims his marble at James's and that other boy shouts, "Keepsie," as his marble ticks James's blue cat eye.

Steph tells me there's a more challenging marble game with three small holes spaced three yards apart. Both players take three turns aiming for holes placed close to the edge of the pavement. If a player doesn't sink the marble in the hole, the opponent can click the outlying marble and knock it further away.

"Steelies can really knock marbles away and are legit, but even Da doesn't have those at our store."

Just then Mrs. Leib calls, "Time to come in for the night!"

Minna smiles and skips in the door holding Ruth's hand.

As fun as the marbles were, still, I want to be settled with my family. I want to be a kid in school in Warsaw. I want to walk home to my mother's warm poppy seed cookies. I want to hear Minna giggle at least half of every day. Then I think about the Gypsy girl I saw leaving Warsaw before dawn and feel guilty, because we escaped and have been cared for by loving people.

I've never shot a gun but I'd be able to do so to protect my sister. I never thought I would feel like shooting anyone, but I know if I need to, I could shoot a Nazi. Steph's such a goof-off he'd be shocked to know how intensely I'd protect Minna from harm.

When we come inside, I notice such a serious expression on Mr. Leib's face. I think he has seen more hatred and suffering than he lets on. He watches over all of us with a wary look. Mrs. Leib says that the Leib family first tried to settle in Northern Ireland, due to an early 1900 program, but Jewish families weren't welcome, so his family moved to Dublin. Steph's grandfather opened the grocery, and then Steph's dad continues the business.

I'm now able to say out loud thoughts that have tormented me for months. Dubliners say what they really think. There are no filters here in conversations. There is no code like Dona Grace and Bubbe's letters rely on. There are no eyes everywhere here in Dublin.

People, even our Jewish hosts, completely relax. When Mr. Leib returns from their grocery store, he and Mrs. Leib go into the living room for a short visit. They laugh and smile. Our home was different with dinner served as soon as Father came back from the store.

Father ate just a little cheese and Mother's bread for lunch at his jewelry store. By dinner time, Father was hungry for dinner, so they visited after dinner. I could hear the quiet conversations between Mother and Father about his day at the jewelry store and Mother's time with her violin students. But I wonder why our family and other Jewish families didn't laugh as openly as the Leib family.

After the girls go to their bedroom, Steph asks his parents if we could take a short walk. Our favorite walk is along the Ha'penny Bridge. We listen as ships come and go. Usually, there's a soft breeze, but tonight there's a biting wind off the water.

"What will you plan to study in college?" Steph asks.

"I haven't thought about the future much lately."

"Ah, sorry, to ask such a personal question."

"No problem." I shake my head. Unbelievable. I must have picked up that Irish phrase from his sister, Ruth.

"We've not been affected by the war like you, so really, I apologize."

"No prob..." I start to say, but then we both laugh. "Actually, I want to be a real artist," I say hesitantly. *Is that a real career before you are successful?*

The off-white color of the bridge blends into the gray sky, but fresh air always feels so wonderful. When we last saw Grandfather in Paris, even air seems to watch us through the billowing clouds.

"Next January, Peter, we'll see the Turner exhibit at the National Gallery."

"Did Turner paint seascapes?" I ask as I follow the lapping water on the Liffey.

"Yes, the light's amazing. It'll be worth your wait."

We walk further across the bridge until a strong wind forces us to turn around.

As we walk near home, a caravan passes us on the street. With the full moon tonight, many people on the front seat are visible.

"What's the driver sitting on?" I ask. The driver appears to be perched on a high box to guide the horses.

"In the front it's called a 'dicky box,' and in the back the platform is called a 'rumble,'" says Steph.

"With their dark hair, this group resembles the gypsies fleeing Warsaw before dawn," I say.

"Here in Ireland the people who live in a community in separate caravans are called 'Irish Travelers,' but they are similar in their roaming lifestyle."

"Hitler rounded up the Gypsies long ago in Poland. Are Travelers in Dublin free from persecution?"

"Mostly, yes, but they like to keep to themselves," Steph says.

From the back of the caravan, I feel the eyes of a girl stare long at me as her red hair flares in the blustery wind. She holds onto the frame of the back door of the caravan.

When the girl's twinkling eyes stare for the longest time directly into my eyes, I feel a sting in my eyes. It's like she enters my heart directly through the intense eye contact. *Have I ever looked at anyone for such a long time?*

I always like to talk to girls, but never know how to kid around. *Will I be laughed at by her? Who is she?* She is beautiful and unusual at the same time. Her clothes aren't like Minna's skirts and blouses. This Traveler girl wears everything fancy, glittering in the moonlight. She wears a shawl and pearls on her neck. Her skirt is long and sparkles. There is something mysterious when a scarf tries to cover wild curly red hair. There're no people I know in Warsaw with red hair.

Steph notices this, too. "Well, I see you've caught a Traveler's eye, Peter, my boy."

That flush I feel from my throat to the roots of my hair tells Steph more than any words could say.

CHAPTER 18

⸺ ◦◇◦ ⸺

Bold Irish Paintings at the National Gallery of Art

"Peter, we're off to the National Gallery," shouts Steph. He bounds toward me after the last school bell rings and we bolt out the door.

"Won't we be waiting until next January to see the Turner paintings? Besides, we need to walk the girls home."

"Oh, I told Ruth to wait for Minna and go home with her today. I told her we need to stay after school to help set up for the spring carnival."

"Sorry, Steph, I don't see going to the Gallery on a week day. We could go on Saturday."

"No, Da needs us at the grocery this Saturday since crates of canned foods are coming in."

"I didn't catch the clue that you enjoy art enough to go to an exhibition."

"Peter, you're a bit thick sometimes! Remember, I told you Annie works there after school. It's not as popular at this time of day during the week. We get to really see each other at this time of day if you catch my hint."

"So, I get to visit the art and you visit Annie?"

"You got it! Let's go."

Annie expects to see Steph, judging by the pleased smile on her face. She winks at us as we walk into the empty cavernous halls.

"See you in an hour, Peter!" says Steph. He holds Annie's waist and they walk to the front desk in plain view with nobody else in sight.

He's clever with girls. Wonder if I'll ever be that comfortable?

The exhibition includes many Twentieth Century artists. *I'm anxious to begin to paint again, but where can I paint in the Leib house?* I turn back to ask Annie where the Turner paintings are. *Maybe Steph is mistaken about the exhibition.*

"Sorry, Peter, you'll have to wait until next January. The Turner donor requires Turner's paintings only be shown in January to preserve the paint from sunlight. Instead, you could go to the second gallery floor where there is some contemporary art."

The first painting is "Girl with a Red Ribbon" by Gabriele Munter, a German Expressionist painter. The girl's dark fixated eyes remind me of Minna's eyes for the past months. Since leaving Warsaw, Minna's eyes reflect only confused tension. Her eyes are no longer the eyes of a child. Sometimes, I know I feel younger and more curious than Minna.

"Decoration" is the next painting that draws me close enough to read the label: Mainie Jellett from Ireland. She's only twenty-six, but her cubist art draws admiration from some critics and hostility from less adventurous who are critics of the new abstract art.

My favorite, as I check the time on the clock and know I'm almost out of time, is "Alongside the Liffey Swim" by Jack B. Yeats. Energetic swimmers are in a race in the Liffey River. I've grown to love watching the water in the middle of Dublin. We arrived in Danilo's boat on the Liffey. Forever, I'll remember it.

"Peter, time to go. The Gallery's closing now. They're firm on everybody leaving. We get to walk Annie to the corner for her trolley." Steph reaches to hold Annie's hand.

"We?" I thought, as we leave for dinner at home.

After dinner, dishes are left to the four of us kids.

Danilo knocks on the door and says, "I've a letter from your grandmother. Dona Grace contacted me a month before, so the news isn't news."

Again, there is a long time between Danilo's visits.

"So great to see you and Minna fitting in with the Leib family," Danilo remarks as he glances at Minna near the front door.

It's true that Minna smiles more, and she even holds Ruth's hand on the walk to school most days. I don't feel like my jaw's clenched as it was many days in Lisbon. Eyes are not everywhere here, but I still feel wary sometimes, as if someone were watching me just out of the corner of my eye.

"This is for you and Minna, Peter. I'll step into the kitchen, so you and your sister can read your grandmother's note."

I shrug my shoulders as I connect with Danilo's eyes.

"I'll leave you and Minna some privacy, Peter," says Mrs. Leib.

"Thank you, Mrs. Leib," I say, as she turns and closes the kitchen door to give us complete privacy.

I slowly tear open the letter, but decide before beginning that I'd glance a sentence ahead. I read more slowly than usual, so as to skip any news that would upset Minna. So far, the first sentence is just general conversation.

Dear Minna and Peter,

We are missing you both, but trust that you are settling in with the Leib family. We only have been told of their happy home. Is school interesting, or are students departing as often as they were in Lisbon?

Dona Grace so longs to hug both of you as do I. We have no news from either your mother or father.

Seeing the next sentence, I skip reading the one note:

There are rumors that they have joined each other in Spain.

Please write and tell us about your art, Peter, and Minna's music.

All our love, Bubbe and Dona Grace.

Minna bites her lower lip as she thinks of Bubbe's question about music. So far, Minna's music is forgotten. She quickly runs to the bedroom she shares with Ruth.

"How's your journey?" I ask Danilo.

"Oh, a bit rougher than your voyage," Danilo says. He runs his fingers through his shiny black hair.

"Are the waves too much for the boat?"

"Ah, no. We were stopped by the Nazis to check the boat."

I gasp. I never considered that there are eyes watching the Lisbon Run. "Have you been stopped before?"

"No. We're such a small boat, but with the war intensifying and borders closing between the Pyrenees and Spain, we need to take care."

"Did the Nazis find anything?" I say, alarmed, and then whisper. "Anyone?"

"No, we just had fruits and vegetables that we always transport." Danilo looks around slowly as though there could be someone listening to him.

For the first time since Danilo brought us to Ireland, I feel a shiver of fear.

"Not to worry, Peter. Sorry to scare you. It's difficult now in Portugal. The enforcement of the thirty-day-stay before deportations is now strictly enforced, so all of us feel pressure to worry for those who are trying to escape."

"When our coaster was stopped, sailors lined up with their tattered clothes contrasting with the grey-green uniforms and those always shiny clunky boots the Nazis wear. One of the sailors tried to remove the moss from the toe of his boot on his other leg as he glanced at the gleaming Nazi boots in front of him. Boxes were kicked aside and two boxes broke as the Nazi holding them seemed to lose his grip. From the way he held the box, it was obvious the box was not heavy. They were trying to terrorize me and the captain."

"My grandmother's letter mentions a rumor that my mother and father are together. I didn't read that sentence out loud, because I don't want Minna to get her hopes up yet. Do you know if this is true?"

"I haven't heard such a thing, Peter, but please take care in sharing this information with anyone else. It's too easy for a careless slip of information to cause incredible difficulty. I need to leave you now, because we probably will be checked again on the return to Lisbon. I am so happy we got you here and we didn't have difficulty with Nazis."

Before Danilo leaves, I give him the letter I wrote three weeks ago. Nothing Bubbe brought up would be answered in my return letter, but this is the new way: News is not news and questions are answered too late as well.

Steph knows the letter upset me, since I walk hurriedly back to our shared bedroom and close the door.

"Come on out, Peter," invites Steph. "Tomorrow after school, we'll catch the tour bus for you to really get the lay of the land here. Dublin has beautiful old buildings and green grounds everywhere. What do you say?"

"Steph, you're the best brother anyone could find!" I tell him truthfully. Danilo's comment about my parents being together, but not coming to join us in Ireland, felt like a punch to my stomach. I thought we would be safe until mother and father could join us here in Dublin. Now, who knows? Thankfully, Steph is pushing me to take a break today.

"We'll go to Trinity College—we'll get a guided tour of Trinity. Then, we'll see sights as the bus driver tells quick facts as we wind around town!"

"Sounds great!"

When the last bell rings, Steph doesn't even wait to catch a glimpse of Annie, so we can catch the last tour of the day. We run to catch the bus. At Trinity College, a former music major guides us on the tour.

The walk on the grounds is energizing. Two monstrous oak trees line the entry.

"These oak trees came from Portland, Oregon, in the United States," says Steph as we walk the sidewalk between the two massive trees."

The expanse of the trunks is stupendous. I'd like to rub my palms on the trunk to bring some of the oak's power to myself. I want to sit and paint the monstrous leaves.

Steph adds information the tour guide leaves out: "The second floor includes the philosophy department and the debate team. Here Jonathan Swift, James Joyce, and Oscar Wilde participated and pondered."

Those names are new to me, but Steph when he sees the questions in my eyes adds, "They're great Irish writers."

As we walk into Trinity College, Steph points back to a brown door on a gray stone building across the grounds and tells me that was Oscar Wilde's apartment. We walk through the massive door at Trinity main entrance and down a hall to the display with the *Book of Kells* inside a plexiglass enclosure.

"It's amazing the *Book of Kells* survived the Viking conquest. Vikings burned books like Hitler does," says Steph. Monks recorded the New Testament of the Bible before Norsemen could burn that book.

Our tour guide, Padraig, stands in front of our group. Steph and I are in the middle of the front row of visitors. He begins to tell us that vellum, calfskin, was used for the pages. "You will notice there are human figures and mythical beasts and the Celtic knot. Vibrant color has lasted for four centuries."

I notice the depth of green and red colors. "It's amazing those colors are vivid after such a long time, Steph."

"The *Book of Kells* has gold leaf on the edges of the book," continued the tour guide.

"Upstairs, the Long Room, a high-vaulted wooden enclosure holds busts on one side of scientists and philosophers," gestured the tour guide pointing with his left hand to those busts. Then his right hand points out busts of literary giants.

"Two hundred thousand of the oldest books in Ireland are here," says Steph with a wide gesture towards the floor to ceiling shelves of books. "See at the very end of the room. It's a harp made of oak: This is the model of Ireland you see on coins."

"Has Ruth been here?" I ask.

"Ah, lots of times, but you're right. We should bring Ruth and Minna. Minna would love to describe the harp to your mother."

Back on the bus we wind past the Guinness Factory. "One day, Peter, we'll drop in for a beer," says Steph. His eyes twinkle with the thought of being a young man. He's almost there at sixteen. At fourteen, I've some time to wait. My parents only enjoy a small glass of wine on Sabbath, so drinking is not in our culture like it is here. Pubs are full in the evenings and sometimes in the daytime, as well.

Steph knows how to shift my mind from worry to fun, yet I long for those Paris sidewalks and the voice of my grandfather, as I fall asleep after our long tour day.

CHAPTER 19

I'm a Grocery Worker in Leib's Grocery

Mr. Leib knocks on our bedroom door. "Time to rise, boys!" he shouts in a too-cheerful voice. "Peter, my Saturday helper, Liam, says he can't come in today because he twisted his ankle playing soccer. He won't be able to stand and stock the shelves, so I'm asking for your help, too."

"Glad to work with you, Mr. Leib, but I haven't worked for anyone except my father."

"No problem there, Peter. You'll just follow Stephan in stocking shelves."

Steph grunts, "I'm fagged, Da. We stayed up late talking."

"You've worked every Saturday afternoon since you were six, Stephan. Rise and shine! We'll leave in fifteen minutes." He lifts the bottom of the window shade up and it spirals to a stop with a whirring noise. Mr. Leib gives one backward glance to Stephan and walks out of the room.

I'd been to the store once before, just to visit with Steph as he waited on customers.

"The canned goods that come in on coasters like Danilo's arrive once a month. Produce from Lisbon comes in twice a month," says Steph. "We'll work non-stop today, Peter."

The Leib's Grocery Store on Clanbrassill Street isn't large, but holds many goods in neat stacks on the floor. Shelves are full of canned vegetables, fruits, boxes of pasta, and tins of meat. The floor is a checkerboard pattern of precise black and tan tiles that were laid when Mr. Leib's father owned the store. There is a large scale to weigh meats and a small scale for produce on a back counter. The cash register is ready for the busy Saturday. Small pieces of hard candy underneath the counter on glass shelves await children's eager *pingin*. Everything is out in plain sight.

The first customer, Dennis O'Leary, comes in and greets Mr. Leib. "How's she going?"

"Isn't this a grand morning?" replies Mr. Leib. He wipes his hands on the spotless white apron tied around his waist.

"How're we so fortunate here in Ireland to still have the pick of the oranges and fresh beef when Paris is starving?"

"Well, since we're not in the War, but in 'The Emergency' with the Lisbon Run operating, everything's still the same for us," smiles Mr. Leib. "Other countries aren't so fortunate, there are extravagant charges even for bread."

I hadn't thought about Mother starving in Paris. She wrote about standing in queues for foods and the Nazis buying up delicacies, but I didn't think deeply enough, obviously. My throat feels dry and I wonder if I'd be able to enjoy tonight's dinner with Minna and the Leibs.

The small bell above the door rings and there she is: the wild-haired girl, with a woman. *Maybe her mother?*

"Good day to you, Kathleen," says Mr. Leib.

"It's a good day, Mr. Leib," said the Traveler.

"What would you like today?"

"I'm having guests for tea and would like some of your wife's apple cake."

"Mrs. Leib made fresh cakes this morning. They're popular for Sunday dinners," says Mr. Leib with a direct eye to stop me from me staring at the Traveler's daughter.

"The thinly sliced apples are just perfectly tart," Kathleen replies and smiles as though she tastes her favorite treat.

Steph says, "Hello, Maeve. I don't think you've met my friend. Actually, he's my brother by choice, Peter."

Maeve bows her head to the left as she smiles a half-smile at me. It's like she really knows something about me that

I don't know. Steph told me earlier about the mysterious intuition that many Travelers seem to possess after the first stare she gave me on the road. It is strange that I don't feel nervous meeting her and thankfully that red flush doesn't happen.

"Maeve, please choose a few pieces of candy for yourself." Kathleen breaks into the quiet and prolonged silent exchange between us.

Mr. Leib wraps the cake in butcher paper and ties it carefully as if it were a present as he hands the cake to Kathleen. Maeve and her mother exit the store without a backward glance by Maeve.

"This is the reason I don't close the store on the Sabbath," says Mr. Leib in a hush. "My father, too, kept the store open for the Catholic customers. We observe the rules for our kosher foods, but I wonder sometimes if that is enough. If my father thought Catholics and Travelers were a reason not to close the store, I'll think no more about it."

"Did your father keep his jewelry store open on the Sabbath, Peter?" asks Steph.

"No, there are many Catholics in Warsaw, but most of our customers were Jews."

The day is full, but we take a break for some pastrami and cheese and a wafer-sized slice of Mrs. Leib's delicious cake. On the way home, we make deliveries to customers too old or ill to come to the store, but Maeve is never out of my mind.

Sunday morning, we set out for Phoenix Park! Mr. and Mrs. Leib walk in front of us. They call us "kids" instead of "children."

"Can you believe the cost is still only one coin, Peter?" Faster than their meandering parents, Ruth and Minna skip ahead at a fast clip.

Steph jokes with his parents as we walk to the trolley for Phoenix Park. This huge park's only five miles from Dublin.

"It's sixty-two acres!" says Mrs. Leib emphasizing "sixty."

Steph whispers the tale of the so-called murders of 6 May 1882, in Phoenix Park. "Britain's Prime Minister's personal secretary, Lord Frederick Cavendish, was stabbed on the first day as Chief Secretary of Ireland with surgical tools."

I shudder and am glad the girls are far away from us and don't hear that story.

Then Steph points to the railway line: "This is the Ghost Line." Somehow Ruth and Minna are again at our sides. Ruth on Steph's left side and Minna on my right side.

"Ghost Line?" whispers Minna.

My eyebrows lift since ghosts aren't mentioned in Warsaw.

"Ah, it's just the name of the underground rail line," says Mrs. Leib, who overheard Steph. "Don't frighten the girls, Stephan! Actually, since the War began, emergency supplies of food are stored in the Ghost Line Station."

"Look, Stephan," says Mr. Leib. "Those hooligans are getting a talking to by the Guarda Siochana."

"Peter, no one can carry on in Phoenix Park. There's a morality law here. No smooching in the park. They may be asked to leave by the Garda," says Steph with a wink to me.

"What's over there?" asks Minna, looking at a large oval.

Mr. Leib bends over and grins as he tells Ruth: "The polo matches are played on the weekend. Your old dad even played there."

Steph says, "The motor races are currently on hold until the war ends. So exciting to watch! Back in 1929 the Irish International Grand Prix was held at Phoenix Park. Before my time," said Steph, as though he needed to add that.

Ruth is racing ahead of even Minna toward the zoo. Mr. and Mrs. Leib pant as Mrs. Leib yells, "Catch the girls, Stephan and Peter. They shan't get too close to the cages. The Garda'll be warning them of the dangers."

Ruth first runs to see the tapirs, her favorite animal.

As we catch up to the girls, Minna's reaching into the monkey cage.

"No, Minna!" I yell. "The monkeys have sharp teeth!"

Minna yanks her fingers back just as the baby monkey bites the bar.

"Clank!" rings out, as the monkey's mouth latches onto the cage bars.

"Whew, I'm glad for the warning, Mrs. Leib" says Minna, shaking her shoulders and bringing her hands around her back.

"We walk along the Kazimierz Alley to enter our Warsaw Zoo," I tell Steph.

"I didn't imagine Poland would have a zoo. Is your zoo impressive?" Steph asks.

"It was amazing! There were elephant and giraffe houses and a seal pond. Minna, as you might guess, loves the monkeys, but she never tried to pet one until now."

"Is the zoo still going with the war there?"

"No, the zoo was bombed in September when we escaped. Missiles and bullets killed most of the animals. We heard reports as we raced toward the forest. Father heard Nazis transported the most valuable animals that survived to Germany and others were eaten." I whisper as I tell Steph that the place we so loved is destroyed.

"Come along to the elephant enclosure," invites Mr. Leib. Ruth and Minna bound ahead of us as Mrs. Leib tries to keep up with them.

"Da, I heard from a tour guide last time we came to Phoenix Park that Winston Churchill lived here. Did he really live in the South? Why didn't he live in Northern Ireland with the Brits?"

"Winston Churchill's grandfather lived in Ratra House, and Churchill lived here until he was six. The rumor is, Winston watched hundreds of cavalry men on mounts from the Marlborough Barracks drill daily. As a child, Winston watched more than eight hundred cavalry and mimed their movements. That's why Churchill is such a war strategist," says Mr. Leib, admiringly revealing his respect for one English leader.

Passover Seder Plate, with Six Symbolic Foods

CHAPTER 20

We Go to the Sheffield Fair

It's been good to be in Dublin for the summer and not be afraid of watching eyes like the eyes of that new boy in Lisbon. Even the parents are excited for the Fair. Mrs. Leib tidies the kitchen as we wait, Steph taps the top of the sink, while Ruth and Minna pull aside the lace curtain in the living room to hurry Mrs. Leib. I only rub the leg of my pants up and down in anticipation of the Smithfield Fair. Summer ends, but we now have the Smithfield Fair!

Steph says the Travelers will be there, and I want to glimpse that red-haired girl again. It's been some time since she stole my heart.

"Smithfield Fair's held for hundreds of years the first Sunday of March and again in September. This March's weather is fair and the idea of a huge horse sale, and booths with art, music, and foods is exciting," says Steph.

"Horses are the focus of the fair. Travelers for years buy and sell Cobb horses there. Smithfield Square's close enough to walk," says Mr. Leib.

Minna's excited to hear music and Ruth wants to ride in a cart pulled by a beautiful horse. The girls chatter as we walk down the lane.

"Look at that boy!" Ruth points to the carefully brushed white feathers cascading from the knees of a horse to the ground.

"Who brushes the horses?" Minna asks.

"The owners hire young kids to groom the horses, so the horses sell quickly," replies Ruth. "The color is called piebald: black and white. When the horse runs it looks like a kite in the air!"

"She wishes we lived on a farm or were Travelers so she could own a horse, Peter," says Steph.

"No horses for us," says Mrs. Leib, as we approach the huge gathering.

"You may each spend these coins," said Mrs. Leib. She gives us each three silver coins. "We'll meet back here in one half-hour just to see what each has found to buy. Then we'll break apart again to look some more. It's such fun, Peter and Minna, to show you the Fair."

Minna fingers the coins. The front of the coin showed a deer and the word, Punt, and the back of the coin spelled, Eire, at the top and the year of the coin, 1938, with a large harp.

"I love this harp on your coins, Mrs. Leib," says Minna as she gazes at the strings on the musical icon.

"I love the deer on the front of our coins. Here in Ireland, we have red deer," says Ruth.

"Off we go, Peter, my man," says Steph as he grabs my sleeve and pulls me down the rows of Travelers' caravans.

There are many, so how can we find that girl?

"I know what you're thinking," says Steph.

"No, I'm not thinking any such thing," I lie.

"I'll leave you to her," says Steph, standing next to Maeve. *How did she just appear?* The green-eyed girl again stares into me. Steph gazes back and goes down the street.

"I'm called Maeve for the fierce warrior who challenged Cuchulainn," explains Maeve to my unasked question.

"Who is Cuchulainn?"

"He's the fiercest warrior ever to set foot in Ireland," says Maeve.

"Are you that fierce, Maeve?" I ask. Steph would be pleased I could ask her such a question, but inwardly, I shudder to think of a fierce woman.

I must ask Steph to tell me about these Irish mythological figures.

"Come with me to visit with my mother to learn your fortune," taunts Maeve as she gently touches my index finger.

Her hands are soft and gentle. With her long fingers, she must play a stringed instrument.

Maeve leads me to her mother's caravan. "Our caravan is barrel-shaped: that's the traditional shape for an Irish Traveler's caravan."

"What's the difference between the Warsaw Gypsies and the Travelers, Maeve?"

"Gypsies came from India, and Travelers originate here in Ireland, Peter."

The exterior of the caravan is painted verdant green with vertical scroll lines. Interspersed are strips of gold leaves with green abstract flowers. The door handle's a unique silver elongated door plate with a handle of a dancing nymph.

"Art may be found in jewels as on canvas, Peter. Yes, I remember your name. Hello, Peter. I'm Maeve's mother, Kathleen Murphy, from Galway."

Her mother's black hair is rolled like cylinders underneath a large patterned blue and green scarf. The scarf ties in a bow at the nape of her neck. Her dress is a long and loose purple velvet, unlike the stiff suits most mothers wear now. Her open necked deep v in the front is surprising for a mother. She doesn't look like my mother ever looks.

Inside the dark room, drapes over windows are dark green velvet with golden ties pulling them back, so glimpses of daylight through the window add a mystery. An orb sits on a slender table near a window. In the Torah, orbs are not allowed. I should not be here, but Maeve has me enchanted. Our Rabbi outlawed crystal balls. It was considered taboo. I shiver to think about Kathleen's knowledge of the future, but I need to know the future for Minna and me and my parents.

I can't believe the sensuous fabrics inside the caravan. The colors alone make me blush. I remember home in Warsaw with silver goblets and the cream-colored lace tablecloths. Here it is all brilliant green and lush purple velvet seats on chairs and red lace table cloths. The colors together are like a wild kaleidoscope. You look in one direction and there are triangles of furniture and objects. All the mirrors make me think of eyes everywhere again, but these explosions of color seem more peaceful somehow.

If I can find any hints even of the future, I may plan as carefully as possible to be at least observant of our chance to reunite with Father and Mother. I know for sure, though, it would need to be in Lisbon, or here. The United States was a possibility last year, but those borders seem closed to immigrants.

By now, it is probably too difficult to gain passports, but if Father determines for us to be together, he might arrange such an event. I love the Leib family. They are so decent to Maeve's mother and other Travelers. Steph says some Irish people don't treat Travelers well, saying they are thieves. Mr. Leib keeps kosher groceries for the Jews on North Strand Street, but he enjoys visits with any of the Travelers who frequent his store on a Saturday.

"You wish to know your destiny? I'll tell it to you, but be warned: If you are happy, beware; if you are sad, rejoice."

I'm confused. This sounds like a riddle.

"Ready? Your future is not in Europe. You will marry a girl with a religion different from yours, but you will live a long and happy life with many children with red hair."

I feel the creep of that embarrassing red coming up my neck.

What is that deck of cards on the table next to the orb? Maeve's mother, Kathleen, is shuffling them like a flash of jewels. They almost sparkle. She doesn't hold the cards like they hold the future. She holds them like they might explode.

It's like there's a real heat in the cards even when they are shuffled in a blur.

I hear Minna's hoot and giggles with Ruth joining in.

"Sorry, but I need to check on my sister, Mrs. Murphy. Maeve, do you want to come?"

I couldn't believe how natural it seemed to include Maeve in my check-up on Minna. She and Ruth have not laughed like that recently. The girls must be having fun, but I hope they're not getting into trouble.

Maeve looks out the door and laughs as she sees Minna and Ruth atop one of the smaller horses. They look so happy and this Fair is certainly an occasion in Dublin. All of the smiles on the young boys grooming horses for pay, the blushes on the cheeks of young performers taking their first bows, and seeing Mr. and Mrs. Leib holding hands will be forever in my memory as the best day since we left Warsaw.

CHAPTER 21

Our Dublin Christmas

I've been restless since the Smithfield Fair. Maeve's on my mind more than the facts the teacher writes on the blackboard. Finally, the last bell of the day is shaken by Mr. Flynn. Ruth and Minna now walk home together without our protection. Mrs. Leib thinks Ruth should have more responsibility for her little sister.

"How's your day?" I ask Steph.

"It's too long. Can't wait until summer comes."

"Summer's still one long time away," I say.

"Well, at least we're not on the front of the battles, Peter."

"True. I must be grateful."

As we enter the house, we hear laughter, a fiddle, and a violin. Ruth and Minna play their instruments together keeping time with the taps of their toes.

"You want to 'retune,' Minna," says Ruth.

"What's that?"

"Tune your strings higher, so there is a repeat of a pipe sound."

Minna places her fingers on alternate strings for an unusual sound and Ruth dips her fiddle down near her waist as the bow zips across.

"Why are they playing today?" I ask.

"Their teachers asked if anyone played musical instruments and both Minna and Ruth raised their hands. Now both are invited to play for the Christmas school program."

"Mother would be so excited for Minna to play in the program. Wish she and Father were here."

"Christmas will be fun with Christmas stockings and Mother's beautiful cookies," says Ruth.

"We didn't have stockings in Lisbon last year," says Minna.

"*Daidí na Nollag,* or 'Santy,' fills stockings with candy, oranges, and sometimes small gifts," says Ruth.

"When we wake on Christmas morn, there are stockings on the kitchen table," says Steph.

Not the same as the Catholic Mass in Lisbon, and no *Bolo Res*, the King Cake, but we laugh with Steph, and Ruth, and

Mr. and Mrs. Leib, and Minna loves the juice of the freshest orange ever.

After such a break in her music, it's surprising that Minna's fingers are still confident picking strings. *Wonder when my craving for art will begin again?* I smile remembering Mother and Minna's duets in Warsaw. People'd stop outside our home just to listen carefully.

After the holidays have gone by too quickly, when evenings are dark, a soft sadness comes over both Minna and me. Mr. Leib turns to the BBC program. Some neighbors pin a war map on their walls to follow the battles. Thankfully, the Leibs didn't do this, to protect Minna and me. For me, though, the map was in my mind constantly, but I didn't want Minna to see the number of pins increase and spread out.

Some nights we listen to the gramophone. Mrs. Leib loves classical records, but Steph loves swing. I like any music to tune out reality. In my mind I'm in the Warsaw Philharmonic Hall listening to Mother play the violin, but then reality returns and I know that building, too, was demolished in September 1939.

After dinner, a knock on the door. There's never a visitor in Dublin after dinner. This is family time. Mr. Leib answers the knock by asking, "Who's here?"

"It's Danilo, Mr. Leib. Sorry to arrive so late."

"How was your journey?" says Mr. Leib as Danilo steps inside and nervously shifts his cap from his left to his right hand.

"Thankfully, uneventful! We've not been stopped since the one time we told you about."

"Any news about the Nazis in Lisbon?"

"Things are still edgy with *Estado Novo*. In France, collaborators now strike fear into the hearts of non-Jewish French men and women," explains Danilo. "It is impossible to trust even those you have known for years in both France and Lisbon. War has crept stealthily into churches."

"Do you have any news, Danilo?" I ask as Minna shyly comes out of the bedroom. Ruth joins her and holds her hand.

"Ah, you know how it is," says Danilo as he shifts away from Minna and stares for some time at Mrs. Leib.

"Minna, Ruth, could you come with me to the kitchen to fix a plate of apple cake for our guests and ourselves?" says Mrs. Leib with a broad smile.

Ruth can never pass up her mother's cake. Minna lingers a bit and then joins them in the kitchen.

Mr. Leib excuses himself and says, "I think you may need to talk quietly together, Peter and Danilo."

"Right," says Danilo. He moves to the couch and sits down. He pats the seat and motions for me to sit next to him.

"We must be so careful with information now, Peter."

"Do you have news of Mother and Father?" I ask in hushed tones.

"I needed to come and just tell you what I've heard from Dona Grace and your grandmother, Peter."

"A man in Spain who has been aiding Jews escape over the Pyrenees contacted Dona Grace to help your parents get to Portugal."

"It's still possible to escape?" I ask, surprised that there could be a possibility of my parents joining us later in Dublin.

"Rumors fly about Winston Churchill's concern for the 'parallel victims' of the War, so Jews are following the route designed for downed pilots and prisoners of war. Also, there are doctors who sign fake medical orders to transfer Jews by Spanish Red Cross ambulances."

"Aren't ambulances searched?"

"Only a few such escapes have been attempted so far," says Danilo.

"Until such an escape can be arranged, your parents are staying in a home above a tea room in Spain. When the time is set, a rowing boat would take them to the Bay of Vigo that is only thirty miles from Portugal."

Just then Minna runs in with Danilo's cake, and smiles as he looks at it hungrily.

"You will not believe how delicious this cake is with the sour apples, Danilo," says Ruth.

"I can't tell you when I've seen such a beautiful slice of cake," said Danilo as he takes one large bite and licks the crumbs from his lower lip.

"Thank you for all you have shared, Danilo," I say, quietly, so there will be no questions from Minna.

After Danilo thanks the Leibs and leaves, Steph asks, "Are you OK now?

"Better than I've been for probably for more than a year."

CHAPTER 22

Belfast Is Bombed

Mr. Leib hears a knock on the door at 4 a.m. He answers the door in his white undershirt and pants.

"My God, did you hear about the bombs in Belfast tonight?" asks Jim O'Toole.

"I've heard nothing about Ireland being bombed, Jim. Come in."

"How bad was it?" Mr. Leib asks, as Mrs. Leib joins them at the front door. Ruth, Minna, Steph, and I stumble into the living room. Minna rubs her eyes over and over, trying to wake up.

"It was massive. With the moon nearly full, around midnight, seven German planes flew low, striking Belfast docks and ships. They were direct hits," says Jim.

"Come in, Jim. Have a seat," says Mrs. Leib.

"How could they be so accurate? Why didn't the balloons protect the docks?" asked Steph, shocked that WW II has come to Ireland.

"Belfast is fighting with England in this war," Mr. Leib reminds all of us, stressing "with."

"Is this like the Warsaw bombing, Peter?" Minna asks the question as though speaking in slow motion.

"I imagine it is," I answer honestly and hesitantly. *Does this worry and fear ever end? Lisbon seems so long ago. That was the only place where there weren't aerial attacks and destruction.*

"Were there casualties in Belfast?" asks Mrs. Leib. Thankfully, she doesn't ask about deaths. Ruth raised her right eyebrow, so I know she understood the longer word for death, but Minna doesn't seem to understand.

"The report is some, but not many," Jim answers, trying to shelter the young girls from the harsh reality. "Houses in east and north Belfast were lost."

"Was this on the BBC radio?" Mr. Leib asks.

"It was. I need to go down our street to be certain people are informed."

"Thank you, Jim, for letting us know. I'll turn on the radio to learn what is happening before I open the store."

"Will we have school today?" Ruth asks her mother.

"Sure. It's Northern Ireland's the target," says Mrs. Leib. "Dublin and Eire are neutral. Thank God!"

"Everyone back to bed until the alarm for school," orders Mr. Leib in a harsher tone than I'd ever heard.

Back to bed doesn't mean back to sleep. Steph pulls the pillow over his head. I set my head on my pillow, but there is no sleep. Warsaw flashes in my mind, the running and crying of people toward the forest. I'd not seen bombed buildings and "casualties," but I had smelled and tasted the fallout of the bombs and perhaps blood in my mouth. *Was that imagined? Or was it real?*

Talk at school is scattered bits of fact and questions. We learn there were thirteen Belfast dock deaths. It seems odd that there weren't more bombs dropped. Only four shelters for Belfast citizens because the Ministers thought an air strike unlikely. Belfast search lights were sent to London, since lights aren't necessary in safe Belfast, and London is often the target of the Nazi bombers.

Only nine days later, back came the Nazis to Belfast, but this Tuesday after Easter the strike begins after 10 p.m. Around 180 Luftwaffe planes hit Belfast with highly explosive bombs in heavily populated northern Belfast. For nearly six hours, bombs drop, like a rain of fire.

Today in school after hearing of last night's Belfast bombing, my nerves aren't holding up. When the boy in front of me at school drops his pencil, I jump. He laughs, but I don't. Mrs. Leib turns down the volume on the radio at home because she sees me wince when the commentator uses a strong inflection on last night's report of displaced Belfast residents.

Mr. Bartels begins the class with a description of last night's Belfast attack. "Rubble made it difficult to save those injured or trapped. There were some deceased in the street. Official figures say that nearly 1,000 are estimated to have been lost. Unfortunately, there are reports of looting. People have run out to the countryside to escape the destruction and fear of more bombs. The most dangerous animals in the Belfast Zoo were shot because of the possibility of them escaping with downed fences."

"Why would anyone loot during these attacks?" I mutter aloud.

"It may happen when desperate people have been ignored. Unemployment increased for some years now, and these people now have nowhere to go."

All of a sudden, Mr. Bartels and I are in a conversation. "What will happen?"

"This makes me think of the Great Depression that never ended for so many. For now, there are temporary shelters and centers set up for seventy thousand. It's rumored that some of our neighbors from the North may move to Dublin."

"Is Northern Ireland poorer than people in Dublin, Mr. Bartels?"

"We are living better because of the ports here and our neutral position in the war. Food is available and there are jobs related to stocking and delivering goods to stores here in Dublin, Peter."

Weeks in May went by with the radio constantly on, non-stop rumors, and new people who'd escaped Northern Ireland drifting into Dublin. Mr. Leib says three men came to his grocery to ask about work. He asked each of them to help stock and clean the store, so he could pay them and save some of their desperation.

I feel uncomfortable as an immigrant when people from Northern Ireland face rude comments and hostile stares from Dubliners.

Minna is not playing her violin. Ruth even stops skipping with Minna to school. People seem to be looking toward the sky in sidelong glances. Looking into the sky is always thrilling for me, to see the sun, sometimes clouds, often birds, but now we want nothing to move in our sky.

A full moon appears on May 4. The BBC is still on late that night because Mr. Leib loves having Sundays off, so he turns the volume to a low level. I am still awake because those April bombings shatter my relief to stop looking for eyes and to try to be young while I have a chance.

Mr. Leib hollers when he hears the BBC announce, "There was an air strike on Belfast suddenly after midnight."

"They're at it again! Belfast has been heavily hit. The report is at least 98,000 bombs fell mostly on the industrial area. The death toll is high and more than half of all Belfast houses are destroyed or damaged beyond repair," Mr. Leib shouts aloud.

I hear Mrs. Leib leave their bedroom to join Mr. Leib.

Steph pulls the pillow over his head. Ruth and Minna appear to have slept through Mr. Leib's outburst, and I shudder, hugging the pillow to my chest.

When will this end?

The last days of the school term end after dragging by, minute by minute. It's warm. I've been sneaking out to see Maeve in the grove of trees near her caravan when Steph sneaks out to hold Annie in his arms in the St. Patrick's Park.

Chuppah, *A Canopy Under Which a Jewish Couple*

Stands for Their Wedding Ceremony

CHAPTER 23

31 May 1941

No! It's morning. Outside people stand in clusters—nobody is running. *Where would we run?* The damage came and went. Someone near me cries. *Could it be Minna?* I squat down on my haunches to move bricks from this old woman. Her leg is pinned. She whimpers. Gently, I tell myself. One brick, then another, and the final tenth brick is lifted near the old one's ankle.

She cries when the weight is off and her leg and foot are still attached. She tries to sit first, but can't. I lift her to sit and then she is able to stand. Her old husband is crying. He staggers toward her. She asks my name, but I am scanning in the dark for a shape.

Steph stumbles into the hall through the kitchen, and sees that Minna and Ruth's bedroom is a shell of a room. I see

Steph's outline move through the missing door. *Where are the Leibs?* For the first time, I can't control this fear. I wipe the tears streaming down my cheeks. Usually, if I bite the inside of my left cheek, tears won't come. My heart is crushed with the thought that Father and Mother will be destroyed if I fail to protect Minna.

Looking back into the kitchen, I notice that all of the place mats are set for breakfast. There is a thin layer of dust particles, probably landing when the bomb fell.

Finally, I realize you can never escape bombs directed at Jews.

There is no forest, I tell myself. *This is Dublin. Tonight at 2 a.m., bombs are falling.*

Another bomb falls closer. Bombs scream like that Banshee Mrs. Leib refers to when the deranged man across the way loses it. The whistle, then the explosion. In my mind, it's like the wisp of smoke in Warsaw. *Grab Minna. Run for the forest. Screams! That burning smell. Does heat smell? Yes!*

As I open the front door, the top hinge comes loose and two bricks drop down. The bomb shakes the house, so it resembles a torn rag doll I saw on our race to the Warsaw Forest. Here on North Strand, masses of people group together to stare first down the street, then up the street, their eyes blank, their mouths open. No one dresses for their escape. Cold. There are a few houses untouched. It's like a giant grabbed some houses entirely, others are badly gouged, and the fortunate few still stand untouched.

I look down North Strand. Smoke hangs low and shells of houses are stripped of their insides, but other houses still remain intact. Stepping into the house, I think, *where is Steph?* I reach for his bed. Then for my bed. There are no beds in Steph's bedroom. *Where is Minna?*

Where is the Leib family? Ruth and Mr. and Mrs. Leib must have run out. Where, most of all, is my little sister, Minna? Please, let her be well. Please, let her hands and feet be unscarred. How can I protect her when I can't see her? Where are Mother and Father now? Are they safe in Switzerland? Are they still in hiding in Paris? In Grandfather and Bubbe's apartment? Where is Minna?

Where would the Leibs gather if there were attacks? Father set up our Warsaw escape plan with Mother weeks, no, maybe months ahead of our hasty leave. Oh, of course, the Leibs would meet at the Synagogue down Clanbrassill Street. In Warsaw, Father told us to gather at our wooden synagogue, Gabin, if there were an emergency. Father never considered the Nazis would march right in and shoot Poles in the street, and we would run for our lives toward the forest. I smell the burning in Warsaw. I hear gun shots. *Who was shot?*

Back to now! I must open my eyes. Smoke is dense and putrid. That is a word that sounds exactly right. We did not smell the intensity of the bombs in Warsaw, since the bombings occurred far away on Sept. 8, 1939. Many lives were lost. Sounds of whimpering and louder cries of "help" rattle in the ragged air.

Living with the Jewish Leib family here in Dublin, the Torah is not strictly followed. We don't observe Sabbath, but I'm not sure I miss it. *What good did being an observant Jew do for my father? For mother? For me.*

How did Maeve just appear? She always makes me think of a sprite. Poof! She just appears! Is she really here?

"Ah, Peter! We were all searching for you!" Our earlier kiss still lingers on my lips.

Why have I snuck out of the Leib household to see Maeve? Never would I have done such a thing at home. Steph snuck out to see his girlfriend, Annie. We should have been with his family and my sister.

"Is Minna with you?" I gasp on "you," in case Minna isn't with her.

"People always race for Phoenix Park when there is a trouble in Ireland, Peter."

"Just as Minna and our parents and I did when we scrambled towards the woods with the Nazis' rush into Warsaw."

"You never talk about that, Peter."

"I can't yet."

Maeve is back after first racing all the way to their caravan to ensure her mother was alive. No damage for the Travelers. It is chaos here on North Strand.

To my astonishment, Maeve just appears. I don't really need to make a plan with her. If I think about her, there she is, and here she is when I am desperate. *Where is Minna? Where is Steph? Where is Ruth? Where are their parents? They've been our parents for these sixteen months. They are so kind to me and Mrs. Leib is even kinder to Minna.*

The shell of the house stands. I race to Ruth and Minna's room. There is nothing but the springs on the bed. Mr. and Mrs. Leibs' room doesn't even have springs on the beds. The room Steph and I share is also shattered. The bathroom is still there. The tub has a towel in it, but no dust. *Odd.*

Maeve looks, closes her eyes, and lifts her head to the sky.

"I think Minna was in the bathroom when the bomb dropped. She must have covered herself with the towel in the bathtub. Why else would there be a towel in the tub? Odd!"

"She gets up at least once during the night. Even with Ruth in the room, she is often afraid because she has nightmares."

"Was Steph meeting Annie tonight?"

"Yes. We both snuck out at the same time. I think Mr. Leib knows about Annie and Steph and just doesn't say anything since Steph does not leave often. Here in Dublin young people marry earlier than in Warsaw. Steph knew you and I were going to meet up tonight."

Soon there are ambulance sirens. It's still dark, but then I see a large, very noticeable figure as he walks down the street.

"Who is he?" I ask.

"That's Johnny Forty Coats," says Maeve.

"What's he doing?" I ask as he opens the right side of his overcoat.

"He's probably dazed by the excitement."

"Excitement? Maeve, you've a strange sense of humor."

"No humor, Peter. He is a bit daft, but fun for kids. He's a stash of comic books; he'll let children look at them when he opens each side of his topcoat. He lives on the street, but everybody knows him and watches out for him. He must've found a safe spot tonight."

I'll promise myself to follow the Sabbath if I can find Minna in this rubble. I won't think of Maeve first again. I will do anything to be with my sister again.

We're wandering slowly, afraid to miss Minna or the Leibs.

Steph shouts, "Oh, I'm so thankful, you're here! Have you seen Ruth, and my parents, and Minna?"

"No one," I gasp.

"We need to split up," orders Maeve. "We've looked inside your home, Steph. It looks like they may have run out before the house collapsed," she lies.

"Maeve, we're here," hollers Kathleen. She is walking down the street holding Minna by the hand. "I saw her wandering far from the Leib home. Thankfully, she escaped!" says Kathleen, her sharp green eyes evaluating the destruction of the Leibs' home.

Minna's dark eyes are still bright in the chaos of the night. I hug her until I pinch her arm.

"Ouch, Peter!"

"Oh, Minna. I was so afraid." I still hold onto her shoulders, but take care not to squeeze her so hard.

I needn't worry for long. Kathleen walks up to hold Minna in her arms, but there is a streak of blood on Kathleen's cheek that frightens Minna. Then, Minna runs over and hugs my legs, shaking with fear.

"This is horrible, Minna, isn't it." I tried to calm her by acknowledging that fear was surrounding all of us in the street.

"Bubbe said we'd be safe here. I love Ruth. She has been my sister for more than a year, Peter. Why did bombs fall here?"

"Nobody seems to know why this happened," says Kathleen.

"We must find my parents and Ruth now," says Steph.

Kathleen doesn't look glamorous now. Her straight hair hangs down her back. Her dress looks old and is torn on one sleeve. It looks as though she's already pulled people out from under collapsed bricks.

We never saw the end result of the bombing in Warsaw. The smell of burning clothes, perhaps that strange odor is burning hair, dear God.

People's faces reflect fear and disbelief. We hear screams: "How could Dublin be bombed? Didn't they see the field with 'Eire' cut into hay in huge letters?"

"Who would be able to see that at night?" answers someone in the dark.

"All of our lights are on. Do the Nazis think we want to be bombed?"

Steph runs over to an ambulance, preparing to drive wounded people to the hospital, to look for his family, but they're not in the ambulance.

A Garda is talking to a crowd asking why the Irish anti-bomb employees don't shoot down the Nazis planes.

"We set up searchlights to track the Nazi planes. It was strange they were not in formation."

"Were warnings given to Nazis?" asks a woman in a tattered chenille robe. Only the ribs of texture can be seen in the darkness.

"Three flares in our tricolor, green, white, and orange, and then red flares of warning are set in the air," the Garda continues. "Our men fired on the bombers with inaccurate shots, so they couldn't hit the planes. Then bombers circled the city for an hour. Around 1 a.m. one bomb fell, then another bomb, and another bomb in rapid succession. After one hour one of the remaining planes dropped another bomb at 2 a.m."

"Were other homes, buildings hit?"

"I need to help in the response. I am sorry not to answer all your questions, but I must say, the Strand is the worst area. In Phoenix Park, there is no other damage except to *Aras an Uachtarain*, the President's residence."

Mutterings about the stupidity of the Germans and the lack of protection by the Irish are heard simultaneously.

Digging under the porch of the Leib house, we find lying the bodies of Mr. and Mrs. Leib and Ruth. I pull off bricks and wooden chunks until they are all uncovered, but they are still not there. *Were they trying to escape when the house collapsed?* Some houses across the street are completely untouched. *How does this happen?*

Blood! Smell of blood leaving Warsaw, sight of blood of the bull in Portugal, now blood all over the Leibs. *How will Steph get through this?* Broken glass like the little girls' game at school in Warsaw, "Glass Piece Secrets." There are no secrets here, no altar with flowers beneath shattered glass. Only grotesque faces under bricks! Shards of glass all over the street, and all over the bodies of the Leibs.

After Steph staggers from the back of their home, he walks in slow motion to us. Minna, Maeve, and I are frozen in place.

"No! This can't be! I should never have left to see Annie!" Steph lifts Ruth's right hand and kisses her fingers, his cheeks wet with tears. "No! She is so little. Why did this happen? We never thought our section of Ireland was at war! What will we do now, Peter?"

Minna looks frantic with all the chaos. Firemen are across the street shooting water into the blasted-out windows as smoke shoots upward. Minna shakes her head back and forth when she sees Ruth and Mr. and Mrs. Leibs' still bodies. "How can you take care of us now, Peter?" Minna whispers.

Glancing at Steph crying, I can't believe sometimes Steph makes me want to challenge him. He goofs off in school. He can't wait to see Annie every day after school. He takes shortcuts when delivering groceries to the old ones who can't come to the Leibs' grocery store any more. If I didn't laugh at Steph once in a while, I'd lose my temper. But now I would like to rewind this night and go back to goofing off with Steph. I can't even guess where the wall is where I hide the jewels Bubbe gave me. Those two broaches are extremely valuable. I don't want to walk away, but Maeve will take care of Minna and Steph needs to be with his family. Ambulances are taking survivors to hospitals, and I don't know where the Leibs will be taken.

This is the wall to our bedroom. I reach between the slats that still hold scraps of newspaper insulation, and there is the ancient pearl broach and then the diamond circle broach. My fingers grasp them gratefully. *What will we do? Where will we go? Doesn't terror stop? We may need this jewelry to survive.*

I need a plan. Our flight from Warsaw was not as haphazard as it seemed. Father carefully budgeted monies before acquiring more jewels for their store. Now I know why fewer jewels were displayed. Thinking about this now, I realize Father was buying the best and most valuable jewels for this terrible time. He knew what jewels could purchase.

There is no way to set a plan. I am in charge of nothing. I am treading water going nowhere. Staying in place is the only way for now. We are safe. Hopefully, Mother and Father are safe somewhere. *Where are they?* This question haunts my dreams now as the castles and mist haunted me before. Could they be in Spain as Danilo heard in the rumor?

We are stuck in Dublin. No news from Bubbe is delivered by Danilo. It has been months without Danilo's visit and now the bombing. We need a place to live. What about Maeve's caravan? None of the caravan was touched.

It's like being orphaned twice, but not like Steph's loss of even his sister, and his whole family.

CHAPTER 24

Kathleen Finds a Second Caravan

Kathleen orders all of us forcefully. "We must go to the caravan, Peter, Steph, Maeve, Minna. Everybody is exhausted, and there are many other people to help with the rescues." She must know it is going to take an order to move Steph.

Will Nazis try to invade from the sea? Should we move further north? No, Belfast has suffered terrible bombings. *Are the Protestants as neutral as the Catholics towards Jews? Will Minna be safe with her dark hair and eyes. In the Caravan will we be safe? Will Travelers take offense that Jews are in their community?* I don't know if I believe in man's humanity anymore.

"Mrs. Murphy, thank you for your kind offer. I'll come to your home after I check with our Rabbi about my family's funeral," says Steph slowly.

"Steph, I want to go with you, but Minna's too upset," I quickly say as Minna wanders away with the lost look in her eyes.

"You need to be with your sister, Peter," says Steph, slowly pronouncing "sister." *How lonely he must feel.* We haven't seen our parents in almost a year and a half, but we didn't see them buried. And there is his sister, Ruth, as well— gone forever.

Maeve is silent for so long. Shock is reflected not just in her now-dull eyes, but in her shrunken shoulders. I can't believe how fast life has turned upside down.

"Let's go in to rest," says Kathleen.

How will I stay in the caravan with Maeve so close by? I want to hold her in my arms, but Minna needs my arms around her.

Minna whimpers. It would be better if she shrieked like she did in her early dreams in Dublin. Ruth gave Minna a glimpse of childhood, thank God. *What God?* Oh, my time with Maeve and Catholics is getting to me. *What would Mother think about all of this?*

Kathleen walks ahead of us with Minna.

Maeve told me last night how Travelers are persecuted in some towns in Ireland and the prejudices are sometimes silent, but hurtful.

Maeve says, "I am sorry for Steph, but maybe sorrier for Minna since she's been traumatized twice with bombs. Ah, and you. The one who is tough and never complains. Does your religion allow you to forgive and see only the positive in people, Peter?"

"I'm not perfect, Maeve."

Only, I can forgive myself. Since Nazis invaded Warsaw, I've never once been young again. I thought I could sneak out just once to see Maeve. I want to hold her hand and feel young. *Who should be blamed: the Nazis, the Fates, God? Where is God?* I've prayed and prayed. We don't follow the Torah as closely as we should. Mrs. Leib cooks only kosher, but we don't follow our old Sabbath practices.

Bill O'Donnell runs up to Kathleen, and tells her of the unofficial report about the air strike on North Strand. I stand next to Kathleen but they both ignore me.

"More than twenty dead and more than ninety wounded, but the number of people without homes is more than four hundred," says Bill O'Donnell.

"Where will they go?" asks Kathleen.

"Luckily, the Irish Red Cross set up stations for the displaced. The Charleville Mall Library will become headquarters."

"Who'll pay for repairs or new houses, Bill?"

"Our Neutralization Act provides money, Kathleen."

"I don't see this war ending soon, Bill," whispers Kathleen so Maeve, and Minna wouldn't hear her dire second sight. "Sometimes I wish the gift of a third eye had been given to someone else, Bill."

"We've all been grateful for your gift of fore-warning, Kathleen. That's why you suggested the location for our caravans. You must have seen this bombing. Take care."

Bill waits for Kathleen's response, but she says nothing.

We walk along the dirt road toward the canopy of trees and caravans.

"We're here, Minna," says Maeve, hugging Minna to stop her shaking. "This is our home, now, Minna."

"So beautiful!" says Minna as the kaleidoscope colors blink, inviting her to examine the living room. My eyes linger and dart like the first time I saw Maeve's home. Most surprising is the bird cage that holds a lively parrot. I somehow missed the bird during my first visit to Maeve's home.

Maeve walks over and sings a few bars of "Toora Loora" through the golden bars of the cage. The parrot cocks his head to the left and listens carefully. "Mother sang that song to me when I was little," Maeve says.

"We'll all be cozy and rest here for now," says Kathleen.

"Now? Where else could we go?"

"Not to worry. My neighbor, Danny, left for Galway to visit his family for a few months," Kathleen tells us as she lifts warm quilts from the chest in the corner. "Danny already asked me to check on his caravan. He'd be pleased if you and Steph stay there," Kathleen lifts her right eyebrow and she fixes her eyes on Maeve. "We must be proper even during this 'Emergency.'"

"Thank you, Kathleen." I exhale all of the air I drew in earlier, worrying about appearance for Maeve and her mother. I know Mother and Father would appreciate Kathleen's concern for proper behavior. Young men and women don't stay together until marriage in Warsaw.

"Won't I see Peter?" Minna gasps.

"Ah, yes. We'll have all our meals together. I am so pleased to have more children now. My husband was a fisherman in Galway, but his boat capsized and I've been without him for so long," Kathleen sighs. Perhaps she thinks of long-ago Galway with a husband and baby daughter.

All of a sudden, the parrot named Eon sings out: "Toora-Loora."

Maeve claps her hands. She has a student.

CHAPTER 25

Steph Plans the Funeral

While Steph arranges the Leibs' family funeral with Rabbi Cohen, I'm alone in Danny's caravan. It is not kaleidoscope colors in here. A bachelor all his life, Danny's a tinsmith and keeps an orderly home, but the caravan's dark colors dim my spirits further.

I have not been to a funeral before, but Steph's grandmother's funeral three years before readied him for the careful preparations. Steph raced to Rabbi Cohen to plan for a *shemira*. "My Rabbi will arrange for a person to sit with my parents' and Ruth's bodies until the time of the funeral," Steph tells me when he returns to our caravan.

"It will take more than the normal twenty-four-hour usual time for a Jewish burial, but the beginning of the funeral preparations is set. Our Rabbi ordered a funeral car to take my family to the synagogue," reveals Steph.

Steph shudders when he tells me the preparations. "Great care is taken for the body of the dead. First, the body is washed and dried and wrapped in *a kittel*," he says, trying not to cry, thinking of all of his family now gone.

He sees my question in my face and answers, "A *kittel is* a white shroud."

"I want to come to the funeral, Steph, but I don't think Minna should come, do you?"

"It might break her heart a bit more if she comes, Peter," says Steph.

"What is the ceremony like?" I ask.

"We'll meet at the synagogue. Before the funeral begins, I'll wear a black ribbon. I'd be honored if you also wore a black ribbon," says Steph.

"Why the black ribbon?" I ask.

"Long ago, the tradition was that closest family members tear their own clothing to represent their grief, and then, wear the shred of cloth for the funeral," explains Steph. "Now the ribbon stands for torn cloth."

"Is Annie coming?" I ask.

"We didn't think it a good idea, since she is Catholic, and they aren't supposed to attend other churches' religious ceremonies."

"Are you sad about this?" I ask.

"Not really. I'm so devastated that I can't feel anything, Peter," says Steph, lowering his head to let hard tears fall.

Reflecting, as Steph regains control, I realize I have never seen anyone cry like this.

Two days later at the synagogue, the Mourner's Kaddish and prayers are said. The gathering is small, but there are enough pallbearers for the wooden caskets for Mr. and Mrs. Leib and dear Ruth.

I loved Ruth as a sister. She was older than Minna and spontaneous and so alive, I can't believe I'll never again see her take Minna's hand and skip down the lane. Ruth will never ride a Cobb horse again.

After the cemetery rituals, Steph and I each dig a shovel full of dirt to throw on the casket.

Each shovel thereafter from mourners causes me to wince and Steph to shake. It is truly the end of the Leibs' life on earth. I wonder what does come in the hereafter. The Jewish religion is not as specific as the Catholics who have visuals of heaven, hell, and some place called Purgatory.

Maeve tries to explain this to me after the bombing, but I don't understand how Catholics can be so certain of specific locations for a person's soul.

"Now Shiva begins," says Steph in a monotone.

"I've not been to a funeral before, Steph. I don't understand the rituals at all," I say in a quiet whisper as many friends of the Leibs remain near the graves.

"It is a seven-day time to try to come back to the real world, Peter."

"What do you do?"

"In the past, the time was allowed for the grievers to regain their wits."

"This is a poor time to regain wits, isn't it?" I ask.

"You are supposed to greet guests in your home, but there is no home. Now—it is gone forever. Just wiped out, Peter."

"Come on, Steph. We'll go see Minna and Maeve and Kathleen. I'm sad this happened to all of you. We loved your family."

There is no Shiva for Steph. On North Strand, it's slow for crews to clear the fallen bricks and metal scraps. Sadness overwhelms us in Dublin. The Garda assist Red Cross workers checking lists of missing people. They wear the saucer shaped metal hats to protect their heads from loose bricks. Reporters with pads of paper note twenty-eight people died and ninety are harmed. Around four hundred are homeless. Luckily,

Kathleen takes us to the Travelers' caravan. Shelters are set up for those without families who can take them in, but it's crowded and unsettled everywhere on Strand.

On June 5, 1941, a funeral mass is said for twelve of the victims. Our *Taoiseach*, President of Ireland, Eamon de Valera, is there to show support. The street is as orderly as a Nazi procession with six men abreast in suits and Garda in uniforms marching to the church.

Along the street, umbrellas cover women from the harsh windy rain, and men in top coats and hats solemnly stand silent. We don't attend the larger Catholic service for Catholics who died in the bombing. *Was Dublin targeted for sheltering Jewish residents and immigrants?*

De Valera speaks, "Although Dublin and Eire are designated as a neutral country, twenty-eight of our neighbors were killed, ninety were injured, and four hundred houses are destroyed. Four hundred are homeless. Let us strive to open our hearts and help one another to recover."

Who is best to care for all of us? Kathleen lives in a Traveler's world. Steph has the business background from helping at Leibs' Grocery, associations with the food distributorship, and international import contacts. He'll be able to help all of us survive.

This could be a disaster now, since events happen too fast. I am stronger than I appear. I think before I act. I need to trust my instincts more. I would like to capture Hitler and make him suffer. I never even killed an ant, but I want to see Hitler cry.

I want to forgive my father for leaving all of us for the jewelry store. We might have been captured; at least, we would have all been together. We may have caused this bombing because we are Jews. *Was the Jewish settlement the reason for the bombing? Don't the Germans know it's the North of Ireland which is on the side of the Allies?*

Steph and I work at Leibs' Grocery every day now. With no school during the summer, both of us run the store. Quite well, I think. Mr. Leib kept clear accounts and records of the suppliers for fruits, meats, coffee, tea, and canned foods.

Kathleen said the other day, "All of Dublin will forever remember your mother's delicious apple cake, Steph."

Kathleen prefers to be called by her first name rather than Mrs. Murphy. "I've not been a Mrs. since my dear husband drowned at sea. We are now family, but I know I'm not your mother, Steph, Peter, and Minna, although I love all of you."

Maeve seems distant now that she is tending to Minna's neediness. Minna wants to always be independent, but now she likes Maeve coddling her.

"Come along Maeve, let's go walk by the Liffey," I invite her one evening while Steph sits in the caravan looking at numbers and costs for the store.

"Not tonight, Peter," says Maeve. "Minna and I are going to teach Eon a new song."

This training of "Eon" is getting on my nerves. *Why does Maeve promise to spend every minute with Minna and that damned parrot?* I plan to walk with Minna and when we return and Minna goes to sleep, Maeve and I can finally be together for just a short time.

Whenever it appears anything is feeling normal, traumatic events occur and I feel more confused than ever before.

As I walk back to our caravan down the road, I hear the faint plucking of harp strings: a sorrowful, few, low notes, and then rushing, glittering, cascading high notes that lift my spirit. Those fleeting notes die so fast. *Who is playing this harp?*

I walk in the dark slowly, lanterns glowing outside closed caravan front doors. Then I see an old woman perched on a stoop in front of her caravan. A lantern sits on a small log close to the harp. Her bent fingers pluck the harp with a large pick.

"Say, are you Maeve's dear friend?" asks the woman in a sing-song brogue.

"I am. My name is Peter. My sister, Minna, lives in the caravan with Mrs. Murphy and Maeve. My friend, Steph Leib, and I are occupying Danny's caravan while he is gone."

"I knew the Leibs well. That bombing was such a shock to all of us in Dublin. Don't the Germans know we are neutral in this war?"

"It was a shock for sure," I answer.

"Do you play the harp for celebrations?" I ask, fascinated by the size of the instrument and the disadvantage she has with her gnarled hands.

"I play just for myself," she answers abruptly as she faces her harp, ignores me. and grasps the pick. Tremulous notes ascend in the dark sky.

Star of David, *a Symbol of Jewish Identity*

CHAPTER 26

Danilo Brings Amazing News

When I circle back to our caravan, Steph is back from the store. His hair is not carefully combed. It looks like he ran both of his hands through it a few times.

"I know. I know. I look like a wreck. I am."

"No, you don't look like a wreck, Steph. But your eyes have circles under them. Aren't you sleeping? I don't hear you tossing. I assume at least sleep comes easily after working so hard at the store all day and balancing accounts most of the evenings."

"It's a wonder parents ever play or talk to their kids, isn't it? I didn't know how hard my dad's life was. Always, he smiled as people came in and out of the store for one or two items, just to visit with him. How did he keep everything perfectly stacked and stocked? And, then the damn books."

"Did your dad call the accounts 'damn'?" I ask.

"Nah, he never cursed at all. Mother just baked those cakes and kept everything in order at home. They had a good partnership."

I shook my head in agreement. I am afraid if I add another idea to Steph's mind, he'd break down. Being so exhausted, he hasn't called on Annie since the bombing and his family's funerals.

"Can we take an hour after we close the store for you to catch Annie leaving the Museum?"

"I'm not ready to step that far into the real world yet," Steph is once again running his whole hand through his hair.

He must have picked up this new habit from worry and sadness. "Do you want me to go and just say, 'hi' for you?"

"Maybe another day, Peter. Thank you for your kindness, but I don't think I can care for anyone again. I loved my family deeply and my heart is nicked. Will I ever return to the real world? Seven days of Shiva have not opened the door to the real world. Every night I hear bombs and smell the awful explosions. How long did it take for you to sleep well?"

Should I tell him the truth? No. He's too knackered for that. "It took until we lived with Dona Grace for the first month. If I'd have known we were supposed to leave after a one-month stay or be returned to Poland, I'd have never even shut my eyes."

"By the way, Steph, I met a woman playing the harp outside her caravan down the road."

"What's her name? How young is she?"

"She's old enough to have arthritis in her hands, but her playing sounds amazing," I'm still confused by her language as I left. "It was strange how she wanted me to leave her alone to play after speaking so well of your family. And she began speaking in a different language."

"That's called '*Shelta*.' It's based on Irish Gaelic and English grammar. I'll tell you the truth, Peter, until my parents, and Ruth, and our house were gone, I didn't begin to understand your strength to care for Minna and keep going day after day, not knowing where your parents were."

I make up my mind to drop by and see Annie somehow tomorrow to ask her to go to Leibs' Grocery. Steph must stop Shiva and reenter the world even if the month of mourning would be cut by three weeks.

How will Danilo find us with the Leib house gone? He'll probably get the address for the Leibs' Grocery from one of the suppliers of canned goods.

"Are the supplies returning to normal?" I ask finally, to make Steph think of practical concerns.

"Not all of the supplies are delivered, Peter. I think the suppliers are concerned about our customers' loyalty, with Da deceased. Also, they are probably concerned that I'm not capable enough to run the store."

"It may take some time to recover the business, but we'll do it!"

A knock on the door of our caravan startles even Steph. Danilo stands on the top step with a large packet of information in his hands.

"Sorry to arrive so late, Peter and Steph. Your parents and grandparents are frantic after the bombings. How are you faring?"

"We're all in shock," says Steph.

"Where is Minna?" asks Danilo, noticing only Steph and I are in the caravan.

"How'd you find us?" interrupted Steph.

"You'd be surprised how many people keep tabs on your families."

I am pleased that Danilo includes Steph's family as well as mine, but it still is reality that only Steph is a Leib in Dublin.

Steph is unaccustomed to the idea of surveillance in Dublin. I forgot to notice eyes in Dublin before, but never again will that be the case.

"Minna is with Kathleen Murphy and her daughter, Maeve," I answer.

"Peter sneaked out to see his girlfriend, Maeve, and I sneaked out to see Annie the night of the bombing," says Steph, still in shock, wishing he could have saved his family if he hadn't been with Annie.

"So very sorry to learn of your loss, Steph. Your parents and your sister Ruth were so wonderful to Peter and Minna."

"The bombings have changed everything," says Steph. "I'm seventeen, not sixty. Customers don't understand that my Da took over the Leib Grocery at fifteen when his Da died."

"I trust you will prove yourself quickly. Peter will enjoy learning the trade as well," says Danilo.

Danilo surprises me when he says, "Peter, your parents have secured passage on a ship from Lisbon."

"They're in Lisbon? When will they come to Ireland?" I can't wait for the answer. I speak so quickly, I startle Steph.

"The routes are closing except for Jews with unlimited monies and the right connections. They're not yet in Lisbon.

They'll be there close to the date of their departure to the United States."

"So, we won't leave with them?"

"The thirty-day limit of stay in Portugal is closely monitored now. Salazar and the pro-Nazis in Lisbon are watching the ports too carefully now for me to take you to Lisbon or for your parents to try to come to you. Coasters are stopped regularly and searched."

My whole body shakes violently to know how close they are, and yet, we can't join them on the ship to the new life.

Steph recognizes my intense fear and tries to change the conversation. "I haven't asked if you'd like a cup of tea, Danilo. Would you?"

"Steph, that would be delicious. I'm a bit chilled tonight. It's not yet full summer, is it?" Danilo rubs his hands on his crossed arms.

I sit stunned and intensely sad. *How will we ever join our parents?*

"I would hate to leave you alone anyway," I say to Steph, but he knows I'm torn by loyalty to this "almost" brother and my yearning to reunite with my parents. It's been many months.

Steph pours a cup of tea and tells us, "I'm going to see Kathleen and give you privacy." Danilo is silent for a few minutes.

Finally, after Danilo gulps his tea, his nerves affected by the tension, he begins to explain how Jews are leaving for the United States.

"A boat called the *Serpa Pinto* takes passengers in eleven to twelve days across the Atlantic," explains Danilo.

"Don't the Germans try to stop the boat?" I ask, fearful for my parents.

"They aren't on a schedule that is known by many. The cost for the Joint Distribution Committee, called the JDC, is over $150,000 to nearly $300,000 for the passage."

"How will my parents get to Portugal?" I ask, dreading the answer.

"They may leave Marseille legally to travel to Portugal."

"When will they leave?" I ask.

"There isn't a set date yet, Peter. May I tell your grandmother and Dona Grace how you and Minna are surviving the bombing and those terrible deaths of the Leibs?"

"It brought back too vividly the terror of leaving Warsaw, Danilo. I could smell those foul odors, and then finding the Leibs' bodies..." I can't continue speaking or thinking about the destruction.

"Ah, Peter. I don't know when all of the terror will end. Why do countries do this to each other?"

I know it is because human beings are greedy. Countries without all of the natural resources want what other countries take for granted.

"How is Maeve getting on, Peter?" asks Danilo.

"We're just a bit apart by four caravans, Danilo. Let's go say hello to Kathleen, Maeve, and Minna," I say.

Minna immediately tells Danilo, "I want you to meet my friend, Eon, Danilo."

"Who's Eon? A new friend, Minna?"

"No, Eon is our special singer!"

"I don't see anyone," Danilo looks confused as he glances around the living room.

"Toora-loora," Eon squawks.

Danilo's eyes fix on the bird cage and he laughs. "You got me, Minna. I really thought you'd lost it!"

"Don't you cry," intones Eon in a melodious tune.

"Are you amazed?" Minna asks Danilo.

"That I am! Your mother will be so pleased with your great progress as a teacher."

"You sound like you know our mother," I state, but I also ask a question.

"Let's step out for a breath of fresh air." Danilo tugged at my shirt sleeve.

"You look like I look when I see Maeve, Danilo."

"I couldn't tell you until now, Peter, but your mother is pregnant."

"Mother pregnant? She's a bit old isn't she, Danilo?"

"No, she's only in her mid-thirties. Women may have babies until they are in their forties."

"Is she ok? Is Father with her?"

"Yes, and yes. They stayed in Lisbon until July to sail for America."

"They didn't come to see us? I can't believe one of them didn't come."

"Your mother was having a difficulty with pre-eclampsia."

"What's that?"

"It's a condition maybe because of her age, Peter, but it's OK now. When they board the boat with other Jewish families, your father convinced your mother that it was best for her to find a doctor and a hospital. They couldn't risk the eyes in Lisbon with a Jewish mother and child in Portugal."

"How can they get out of Portugal?"

"The ship, *Serpa Pinto,* will transport them to Stanton Island, New York. When a company, The JDC, situated in Lisbon, purchased all the passenger seats for refugees, your father booked their passage. The cost of $180,000 and up was guaranteed by the JDC," said Danilo.

"I wondered why no concern from Bubbe or you came after the Dublin bombings." I still feel deep sadness that no one cared about our safety.

"Plans were being made for their departure of June 12, 1941. It only takes eleven days to reach New York. Your grandmother sends you her well wishes and will join your parents in New York soon. Your mother's pregnancy is going well. You will have a brother or a sister in the new year."

"New York? Are we ever to see each other again?" I ask in a gasp.

"I believe you will, but it will take some time," Danilo said.

CHAPTER 27

Our Second Dublin Christmas

Again, it's Christmas without traditional Hanukkah, but we've been there before, in Portugal and then our first Christmas in Dublin. I wonder if Bubbe and Dona Grace will be excited to see the baby Jesus placed in the creche on Christmas Eve. Dear Bubbe and wonderful Dona Grace, who would have been an amazing grandmother, made Minna and me so welcome in her home. She is still Bubbe's best friend after a forty-year gap. *Will Steph and I be friends forever?*

The Leibs' Grocery Store is stocked with oranges for children's stockings. The Irish love to make fruitcake with dates and nuts and soak the bread in whiskey after it is baked. After the Dublin bombing last May, Stephan hands Kathleen his mother's famous apple cake recipe. In September, Kathleen began making the fruitcakes for the Leibs' grocery.

"Your father was so wise to stockpile white flour, Steph. It is nearly priceless with Christmas baking," says Kathleen, cradling the flour as if it were a baby.

Dozens of loaves wrapped in cheese cloth hold in the flavor as the aroma seeps out. She baked the loaves in October to allow plenty of time for the whiskey, spices, and fruits to meld. Steph and I are in the store every day: He goes to classes in the morning while I work, and then we switch. I doubt if Mother and Father would approve, but we need to support five people.

Steph answers customers' questions when they buy the newest ornaments for their Christmas trees.

"What's with the cardboard hangars on the ornaments, Steph?"

"Since the war broke out, ornaments no longer have metal caps and hangers on the top of ornaments because all metal is saved for planes," says Steph.

"The Corning Company puts out over 300,000 ornaments a day instead of the glassblowing rate of six hundred a day," says Steph to Kathleen. "No longer are there silver glass ornaments; instead, tinsel snippets are placed inside the clear ornaments for sparkle."

"Wouldn't you know," sneers Kathleen, "Hitler has even taken the sparkle from our Christmas trees!"

Maeve and Kathleen take three fruitcakes for the five of us for Christmas. After those Nazi bombings, people are eager to pretend life is safe again. The store owners on Grafton Street outdo themselves with window displays this year, according to Maeve.

"You need to see this fantasy window with icy blue drapes under arches. Steps under the center arch display a girl in a huge hooded ocean-blue coat holding a candle to light her way. She appears to be in a mystical winter cave. In front of the scene there is perfume in open silver bottles with silver boxes tied in blue ribbon to purchase inside the store."

"Ah, Maeve. You've always loved Christmas more than your birthday," says Kathleen.

"There is magic for sure," says Maeve. "Will you and Peter be coming downtown next Saturday evening for the carols?" Maeve asks Steph, but then she turns to stare at me.

Shall I answer? Steph isn't saying anything yet. I want to see her, so I quickly add, "Will you and Minna come, too?" I guess we all will meet up. So much for time with just Maeve and me.

"I'll bring my fiddle and Minna will play her violin," says Maeve.

I imagine Maeve's intent look on her face with her fingers plucking strings to dance a jig.

"Well, this will really be a treat!" says Kathleen.

This Saturday passes quickly as we restock the canned nuts and fruits for the cakes that some women are still making.

"We'll be off to the forest to cut a tree tomorrow," says Kathleen.

"It's still two weeks until Christmas," says Steph.

"We'll keep it in a bucket of cold water outside, Steph."

"Why so early this year?"

"I've a feeling the weather may turn and be too cold if we wait. Sometimes we get snow here, Peter, and I just must have Scots Pine in every cranny in the house."

When I leave with the delivery for the old ones, Steph counts the day's money and puts it in the black box he brings to our caravan every night.

Kathleen serves corned beef and cabbage for tonight's dinner. Minna and Maeve are so excited to play at the downtown gathering in a week that they don't waste one second, when Kathleen announces, "You're excused from the table."

Steph is trying to figure out if we might leave Kathleen and the girls for the night when a knock on the door from their neighbor, Mrs. Casey, asks if she might borrow red food coloring for icing for Christmas cookies. The women chatter in the living room as Steph tells Kathleen we need to walk outside for a bit after standing and stocking all day inside at the grocery store.

After the caravan door closes, I ask Steph, "How will Annie know you want to arrange a date?"

"We'll drop by her house," Steph answers. "I want to take Annie to the Metropole Cinema."

"What's the name of the theater?" I ask.

"Lyceum Picture Theater," Steph answers.

"What's showing? We've not been to the cinema since we came to Ireland."

"It seems busy all the time and frankly I'm not that interested in lovey stories. Did your family go to movies every month in Warsaw?"

"They didn't think many shows were suitable for Minna and they didn't like to waste money ever."

"You should be glad for lots of reasons." Steph's face let me know the Leibs' Grocery is not doing as well as it was before the bombing, and before we are running the store.

"Back to your question about the movie. *Fantasia* is one of those movies an intellectual girl like Annie will love."

"What's it about?" I ask.

"Don't know, but it's Walt Disney so no objections should come from her parents."

"Do you enjoy movies?"

"You aren't familiar with the set-up of the theater, Peter. It's dark. There are special seats in the theater. These are similar to orchestra seats. You must have been in opera houses with your mother's orchestras? Maybe the Disney movie will be too bright with all those colors and I won't be able to kiss Annie as often as I'd like."

"Will you still go to that one or will you try to find a movie that won't have such bright lights on the screen?"

"No. It's one of those types that parents don't mind. No kissing on screen. Parents think that influences children. Like we need inspiration," says Steph with a laugh.

Normal? Are we teenagers like teenagers anywhere else? When will I see my parents? But for now, we are warm, happy as can be, and safe with Maeve's mother, Kathleen.

Steph said, "I'm off to check if I locked the grocery. My mind wasn't on work today." Steph runs back.

Maeve is still mostly distant in thoughts. I'm also thinking in rapid-fire fashion: *What will this next year bring? A new baby? What's next?*

Ten Commandements

Manuscript at the Bibliotheca Rosenthaliana, Amsterdam

SOURCES FOR IMAGES

Commons, https://commons.wikimedia.org/w/inde
x.php?title=File:Gastronomie_juive_en_%C3%89g
ypte_(cropped).jpg&oldid=544576863 (accessed
October 22, 2024).

Chuppah. Photograph by Colleen Clancy Hansen, "The   177
Exhibition of the Jewish People," Butte Archives,
Butte, Montana, 5 Nov. 2019.

Star of David. Photograph by Colleen Clancy Hansen,   203
"The Exhibition of the Jewish People," Butte
Archives, Butte, Montana, 5 Nov. 2019.

Ten Commandements. Photography by Ardon Bar Hama.   220
Manuscript at the Bibliotheca Rosenthaliana,
Amsterdam HS.ROS.PL.a-33. Colophon in the
bottom right corner reads, "Written by Jekuthiel
the scribe son of his honor Isaac the scribe. A.M.
5528". In the bottom left, "I wrote this as instructed
by his honor the great and powerful Rabbi Levi
the son of his honor the pleasant Samson
Barkoum Z"L"., Wikimedia Commons
contributors,
"File:0001FL9694984.jpg," *WikimediaCommons*, http
s://commons.wikimedia.org/w/index.php?title=Fil
e:0001_FL9694984.jpg&oldid=885780596 (accessed
October 22, 2024).

ABOUT THE AUTHOR

Colleen Clancy Hansen holds a bachelor's degree in Secondary Education with an English major, a speech/drama minor, and a Master's Degree in the Art of Teaching. She retired after teaching secondary English for twenty-five years at Billings Central, CR Anderson, and Helena High School. Since 2006 she has been a member of the Society of Children's Book Writers & Illustrators (SCBWI). Colleen published *Destination: Butte, Montana, Ghost Children in Elkhorn, Montana,* an eBook, and *Stella and the Bubble Man,* a picture book. Colleen's newest book is *Eyes Everywhere: Searching for Jewish Children,* published through Mountain Pine Press (2025).

Contact Colleen Clancy Hansen and learn about her books through her website, www.colleenclancyhansen.com.